HORSE WISE

Meet
The Saddle Club™

Horse lover **CAROLE**…
Practical joker **STEVIE**…
Straight-A **LISA**.

HORSE WISE

Bonnie Bryant

Gareth Stevens Publishing
MILWAUKEE

I would like to express my special thanks to Margaret Smith and the U.S. Pony Clubs. I hope I have been able to do justice to this fine organization. — B. B.

For a free color catalog describing Gareth Stevens' list of high-quality books, call 1-800-542-2595 (USA) or 1-800-461-9120 (Canada). Gareth Stevens' Fax: (414) 225-0377.

Library of Congress Cataloging-in-Publication Data

Bryant, Bonnie.
  Horse wise / Bonnie Bryant.
    p. cm. -- (The Saddle Club ; #11)
    Summary: Although the girls are overjoyed when Max forms a Pony Club, Lisa worries that Carole and Stevie will be jealous when she gets her own horse.
    ISBN 0-8368-1533-5
    [1. Horsemanship--Fiction. 2. Friendship--Fiction. 3. Clubs--Fiction.]
    I. Title. II. Series: Bryant, Bonnie. Saddle Club ; #11.
  PZ7.B8344Hu 1995
  [Fic]--dc20   95-38630

This edition first published in 1996 by
Gareth Stevens Publishing
1555 North RiverCenter Drive, Suite 201
Milwaukee, WI 53212, USA

"The Saddle Club™" is a trademark of Bantam Doubleday Dell Books for Young Readers, a division of Bantam Doubleday Dell Publishing Group, Inc.

A special thanks to Miller's Harness Company for their help in the preparation of the cover. Miller's clothing and accessories are available through approved Miller's dealers throughout the country. Address Miller's at 235 Murray Hill Parkway, East Rutherford, New Jersey, 07073, for further information.

1 2 3 4 5 6 7 8 9 99 98 97 96

Printed in the United States of America

For Judy Boehler and Gwen Schmitt

CAROLE HANSON HUMMED to herself as she removed her horse's bridle and hung it on the hook
by the stall door. Then she began unbuckling the
saddle. The horse, Barq, stood patiently while she
worked, as if he knew what was coming. Carole
patted him affectionately. She liked what she was
doing, as she liked everything there was to do with
horses.

Suddenly she heard a grumbling noise. Was it
Barq? Carole stopped humming and looked at him
with concern. If he'd made that sound, then something was very wrong. She might even have to call
the vet. She heard the grumbling sound again.

Carefully, Carole put her ear against the horse's
belly. She didn't have a stethoscope, and if the horse
was really having a stomach problem, she would be

able to hear it better this way. There was no sound, except . . .

"Hey, Carole, I've heard of getting close to your horse, but aren't you carrying it a little too far?" A familiar voice snickered.

Carole straightened up and glared at Veronica diAngelo. Veronica rode at Pine Hollow Stables with Carole and Carole's two best friends, Stevie Lake and Lisa Atwood. But Veronica was definitely not one of her best friends. She was a spoiled little rich girl who cared more about her expensive riding clothes than the health of her horse.

"I thought I heard his stomach grumble," Carole explained. Veronica didn't deserve an explanation, but Carole couldn't help herself. She was a natural-born teacher when it came to horses and riding and was always eager to share her knowledge with others—even lost causes like Veronica. "See, if his belly's grumbling, it could be the start of a colic attack, and that's serious, because—"

"What you heard grumbling was your friend Stevie," Veronica rudely informed her before disappearing toward the locker area.

Carole peered over the stall door to see what Veronica was talking about. Stevie was standing in the hallway with her horse, patiently cleaning Topside's hooves. But the noises she made as she was working weren't patient at all.

"Grrrr," Stevie grumbled, unaware that Carole

was watching. "I hate it, I hate it, I hate it." She swept her dark blond hair back from her face and concentrated on her work.

"You hate cleaning hooves?" Carole asked.

Stevie looked up at her friend. "No, I hate school," she said. "It's only three days into the new semester and I already have seven impossible things to do, including one especially horrible science project. If I don't keep up with school, Max won't let me ride, and if I can't ride, what's the point of school? I just wish they'd teach us about horses in school instead of all this other garbage. Then I'd be a straight-A student."

"Did somebody mention me?" Lisa asked, joining her two best friends. Stevie and Carole laughed. It was accepted among them that Lisa was the best student, just as Carole was the horse expert and Stevie was the best at jokes, practical and otherwise. But when it came to loving horses, they were all equal.

"Yeah, I did," Stevie said. She bent her head and resumed cleaning Topside's hoof. The stone that was wedged under the horse's shoe came loose and dropped to the wooden floor of the stable with a satisfying thunk. Stevie grinned triumphantly at the sound and looked up at her friends. "It's this horrible science project. What do you know about osmosis?"

Lisa looked thoughtful. "Well, it's the tendency

of a substance to pass through a semipermeable membrane from an area of higher concentration to an area of lower concentration."

Stevie sighed. "Does that mean if I put my science textbook under my pillow, all the knowledge will transfer into my brain overnight?"

"Only if your skull is semipermeable," Lisa informed her.

"Wait a minute. I'm the one who tells the jokes," Stevie said, laughing. She unhooked Topside's cross-ties and led him toward his stall. Her voice turned serious. "But jokes won't get me out of this one."

It sounded to Carole like trouble was brewing. She considered the situation as she returned to Barq's stall to finish grooming him. Max Regnery, who owned the stable, had a strict rule that all the young riders had to maintain a good school average. Stevie had always found a way of just getting by, skirting disaster throughout the school year, but Carole was afraid that sooner or later her friend's grades would drop just a bit more than Max liked. Then Stevie wouldn't be allowed to ride until she brought her grades up.

As far as Carole and her friends were concerned, not being able to ride was the worst possible punishment. The three girls loved horses so much that they'd formed The Saddle Club. So far they were the only full-time members, though they had some friends who lived out of town who were honorary members. The club had only two requirements for membership: the members had to be horse crazy and they had to be willing to help one another out. Since they'd started the club, they'd shared many wonderful riding experiences—and they'd had a lot of opportunities to help each other.

Carole thought that Stevie's problem might be the beginning of another Saddle Club project. She peered into the stall next door, where Stevie was beginning to groom Topside. "I think we ought to have a Saddle Club meeting after we're finished," Carole said.

"Great idea," Stevie agreed. "But I don't know about Lisa. Is this piano-lesson day?"

Carole couldn't see Lisa, but she knew where she was. Pepper's stall was three down from Barq's, on the other side of the walkway. "Hey, Lisa, is this piano-lesson day?" she called.

"No, that's Thursday," Lisa called back from the stall.

"Then I think we need to have a Saddle Club meeting after we're done with the grooming."

"Super," Lisa said. "Let's meet at TD's in about half an hour." TD's was their favorite, and most fattening, hangout. It was an ice cream shop, officially named Tastee Delight. The Saddle Club always abbreviated that to TD's. "Now," Lisa continued, talking to herself, "if only I could get

this darn saddle off fast so I could *start* the grooming!"

"Saddle Club to the rescue! I'll be there in a minute," Carole told her friend. She quickly finished the
last of Barq's grooming and left the stall to help Lisa.
Before she could get to Pepper's stall, however, she
found herself once again face-to-face with Veronica
diAngelo.

"Saddle Club?" Veronica asked. "What's a Saddle
Club?"

Carole was speechless. It occurred to her for the first
time that she didn't know if The Saddle Club was supposed to be a secret. She hadn't been thinking about
secrecy when she'd yelled to Lisa. She'd only been
thinking about Stevie's science project and Lisa's saddle.

"I mean, is this some sort of thing the three of you
cooked up while you were at that riding camp?"

That was just like Veronica. The little rich girl
didn't know what to do when other people had things
she didn't. Veronica was actually jealous that the three
other girls had gone to riding camp. She envied their
adventures there. *If only she knew,* Carole thought to
herself.

Veronica stood squarely in Carole's path, hands on
her hips. She made it impossible for Carole to evade
either her or her question.

Carole put her hands on her own hips, stared Veronica straight in the eyes, and spoke. "Your lipstick is smeared."

Involuntarily, Veronica's hand went to her mouth, and in that instant Veronica lost the standoff. She ducked and slithered past Carole, heading, no doubt, for a mirror. Carole continued on her way to Pepper's stall.

"Nice work!" Stevie called after her.

"Piece of cake," Carole acknowledged breezily. Then she walked into Pepper's stall. There was a lot she wanted to tell Lisa about untacking.

As it turned out, by the time the girls got to TD's, there was a lot more than a science project to talk about. They had to consider the meaning of what they'd already come to think of as The Letter. Within a minute and a half of their arrival, they'd ordered their sundaes and solved the problem of Stevie's science project.

"Of course I'll help you," Lisa said. "Now let's get to the other thing."

"So what do you think this is about?" Stevie said, holding The Letter in her hand. It was a note Max had given to every young rider as she or he had left Pine Hollow after class, announcing a meeting for all riders and their parents the following Tuesday.

"I hope there isn't going to be some horrible change at Pine Hollow," Stevie said.

Lisa looked upset. "Oh, I hope not," she said. "I like Pine Hollow just the way it is. I don't want Max to change anything."

"It might be something really great," Carole said. She was always optimistic when it came to riding.

"What could be great that has to do with our parents?" Stevie asked. That was a good question.

"Maybe it's something simple, like a new schedule," Lisa suggested.

"We wouldn't have to have a meeting for that," Stevie told her. "But we would *have* to have a meeting if something drastic was about to happen."

"What do you mean by drastic?" Carole asked.

"Oh, you know, like Max moving to Alaska, or going into the insurance business, or like he's decided not to teach young riders anymore. Things like that."

"That's not just drastic, that's *drastic*," Carole said.

The girls sat glumly, pondering all the awful possibilities.

"Who's got the peanut-butter crunch with blueberry sauce?" the waitress asked. Carole and Lisa pointed to Stevie. She was always ordering the most outrageous combinations. When people suggested she did it to keep others from nibbling at her sundae, she flatly denied it. But it was a fact that no one ever asked for a taste of her sundaes. Even the waitress made a face as she put the order in front of Stevie. She gave Carole and Lisa their orders and the girls began eating their ice cream in gloomy silence. Just when they thought things couldn't get any gloomier, Veronica diAngelo and her friends arrived at TD's. Veronica sauntered over to their table.

"Well, hello," she cooed sweetly. "You three together again? It seems like you're always together. Is this some sort of club or something?"

Stevie gave her a withering look. It didn't have any effect. Subtlety was lost on Veronica.

"What do you want?" Carole asked her, hoping a more direct approach would get her to go away.

"Oh, I thought you'd want to know my good news," Veronica said.

"I'm positively dripping with curiosity," Stevie drawled sarcastically.

"Well, you can switch your curiosity to envy because on Monday, my new horse is arriving."

Carole couldn't help it. The envy overwhelmed her. It was all she could do to keep from showing her feelings. "That's nice," she said with the utmost control. "What kind of horse is it?"

"It's an Arabian. She's a dark chestnut mare and I'm going to call her Garnet. I'm sure you'll all have lots of fun watching me ride her." With those words, Veronica tilted her chin up in her I'm-bettter-than-you—in-fact-I'm-better-than-everybody way and walked off, followed by her cadre of admirers.

"And I'm sure we'll enjoy watching you *not* take care of your horse, too," Stevie hissed at the departing girl.

"This is horrible!" Lisa said. "She rode her last horse

carelessly and he got killed because of it. How can she be getting another?"

"Easy," Stevie said. "All she has to do is to ask Daddy!"

Carole grabbed her spoon and dug into her sundae, trying to hide her hurt and anger. She thought about Veronica's earlier horse, a Thoroughbred stallion named Cobalt. Carole had loved and cared for him more than Veronica had. She'd ridden him better, too. He'd been a beautiful and expensive horse, but he wasn't suitable for Veronica at all, and that had cost him his life. The only good thing that had come out of Cobalt's life with Veronica was his foal—a coal-black colt named Samson who belonged to Max.

"Remember after Cobalt died, Veronica decided she wasn't ready for another horse—actually had to stop her father from buying one for her?"

Stevie and Lisa nodded.

"Well, she's still not ready!"

"Do you think The Letter could have anything to do with Veronica's horse?" Lisa asked.

"I hope not," Carole said. "We'll all be better off if we can ignore this whole thing. So, let's think some more about The Letter. Any other ideas?"

"Yeah—how about Max has sold Pine Hollow to some developers who are going to make a shopping mall," Stevie suggested.

"You're going from bad to worse," Carole said.

"Well, now, wait a minute," Lisa said. "Do you think the mall would have a Gap?"

Carole's jaw dropped.

"I was joking—I was joking!" Lisa said hastily.

Carole liked a joke as well as the next person, but she couldn't find any humor in the idea that something awful was about to happen to Pine Hollow.

"You know, I just remembered something," Lisa said. "When Max handed me The Letter, he had this kind of funny grin on his face. Whatever it is, I think he's happy about it. Maybe we're going about this all wrong. Maybe it's really good news. Remember the time we thought the stable was in trouble?"

"Boy, were we ever wrong!" Stevie grinned at the memory. "We did get a lot of new riders for Max, though, didn't we? Hey, maybe Max has decided to have more riding classes," she added thoughtfully.

"Or maybe more horses!" Carole suggested, brightening.

"Or maybe he's decided to expel Veronica!" Stevie said mischievously.

"Now, that would be more than good news," Carole said. "That would be—" She tried to think how to describe it. "Christmas and birthday all rolled into one!"

"YES, OF COURSE we'll be there, dear," Mrs. At-wood told Lisa at dinner that evening. "The library committee can do without me for one meeting."

"You *will*?" Lisa said, sounding more surprised than she thought she ought to sound. "I mean, this is some sort of meeting Max wants us to be at. It has to do with riding," she added, just to be sure her parents understood. After all, they had never been very enthusiastic about her horseback riding. She couldn't think of a reason why that could be changing so suddenly. "Horses, I mean," she said, to further emphasize her point.

"Is there any other kind of riding?" Her father smiled.

Lisa thought maybe she'd done some unnecessary explaining. "No—it's just that, well, you sort of surprised me. I mean, usually you aren't so—oh, I don't know."

"We'll be there, Lisa," her father said. "Seven-thirty on Tuesday." Her parents exchanged glances.

Lisa began eating her salad. Something was up. She had a perfectly nice set of parents who were usually very predictable. Their eagerness to come to Max's meeting puzzled her.

"I saw Veronica diAngelo's mother the other day," Mrs. Atwood said. "Did you know Veronica is getting a new horse?"

"I heard," Lisa said.

"She told me how wonderful it will be for Veronica to have a horse of her own. You know, owning and caring for a pet like that can be so good for somebody like Veronica . . ."

"To say nothing of the horse," Lisa said sarcastically.

"Oh, yes," Mrs. Atwood agreed, oblivious to her daughter's tone.

Something was definitely up.

THINGS WEREN'T AS quiet or as mysterious down the street at Stevie's house.

"Pass the biscuits," her older brother, Chad, said.

"You've already had three," Stevie's twin brother, Alex, argued, reaching across Stevie to grab the biscuits for himself.

"There's a meeting," Stevie began.

"No, I want the meat first," Chad interrupted.

"What's the meeting?" Mrs. Lake asked.

"At Pine Hollow," Stevie began again. "It's on—"

"Oh, here we go with good old Pine Hollow," Alex teased.

"Sounds like Marsh Mallow to me," Chad added. "Hey—do you think that's Stevie's favorite food because it reminds her of horses?"

"No, I thought she liked to take pills because they remind her of her boyfriend, Phil!" her little brother, Michael, piped in.

Stevie sighed, but she didn't let it show. Phil Marston was her boyfriend from riding camp. He lived about ten miles away and she didn't see him often. She did, however, hear about him a lot from her brothers! It wasn't easy living with three brothers. It was made harder by the fact that she was the only one in her family who cared about horses and horseback riding. Chad had tried it once, but it wasn't because he liked horses. It was because he'd had a crush on Lisa and wanted to get her attention. Now, all three of her brothers seemed to be ganging up on her to keep her from telling her parents about the meeting. As far as Stevie was concerned, that was just the inspiration she needed to persist.

Stevie raised her voice a notch. "I said, there is going to be a meeting next Tuesday at Pine Hollow, after riding class."

"You can go as long as your homework is done," her mother said.

"If that includes her book report on *Silas Marner* from last spring, she'll never make it!"

"Shut up," Stevie said. Only a creep like her twin brother would remind her parents about that book report at a time like this. "I know *I* can go to the meeting. What about you, Mom?"

"Me?" her mother asked, taking the bowl of potatoes out of Chad's hands before he could empty the entire dish onto his plate. "Am I supposed to go?"

"And Dad," Stevie said, looking at her father, who was studying the pattern Michael had made with his squash. Michael often tried to make his food look as though he'd at least tasted it by spreading it around his plate so he wouldn't have to eat any more of it.

"Tuesday, dear, can you make it?" Mrs. Lake asked Stevie's father.

"That's my soccer game," Chad said before his father could answer the question.

"You weren't invited," Stevie said.

"Yeah, but Mom and Dad were invited to the game."

"To watch you warm the bench?" Stevie asked.

"I scored two points last game!"

"Yeah, for which team?" Alex snorted.

"So, I kicked it the wrong way, so? You want to make a federal case out of it?"

There was a second of stunned silence at the table. Then everybody burst into laughter—including Chad, though he had the good grace to blush as well.

"Who are you playing against this time?" Michael asked.

"Same team," Chad said. "Coach said they begged us for a rematch!"

"I'm not surprised," Mr. Lake said.

"Next Tuesday?" Mrs. Lake asked. Stevie nodded. "We'll be there."

Stevie felt a rush of relief. Things had to be much easier for only children.

"NEXT TUESDAY?"

"Yes, Dad, next Tuesday," Carole said.

She and her father, a Marine Corps colonel, were in the kitchen of their house on the outskirts of Willow Creek. It was the home the two of them had shared alone since the death of Carole's mother when Carole was eleven. She and her father both missed her mother terribly, but were glad to have each other to share their sadnesses and their joys. In spite of a few weird habits and hobbies, Carole thought her father was probably the greatest guy in the world.

"That's Navy-Bean Soup Night at the Officers' Club," he said.

Navy-bean soup was one of his weird habits.

"Dad," Carole said with a touch of exasperation in her voice.

"Well, what's this meeting about, hon?" Colonel Hanson asked.

"I don't know, Dad. If I knew, I promise I would tell

you. All I have is this letter that Max gave us. It says we should be there, with our parents."

"Well, I'm not—" He was interrupted by the ringing of the phone. He swept it off the hook and spoke into it smartly. "Colonel Hanson!"

That was another one of his weird habits. He never could seem to remember that when he wasn't in his office on the base, he didn't have to answer the phone that way.

At first, Carole thought the call might be for her, but it was clear that the caller wanted to talk to her father. She turned her attention back to fixing dinner. They were having tacos, and Carole was in charge of making the beef filling. Her father was in charge of preparing the toppings. Carole checked the beef, which was done and staying warm in the electric frying pan. It was time to set the table.

Without thinking about it, Carole took three place mats out of a drawer and put them on the table. When she saw what she'd done, she moved the third mat into the center of the table to use as a hot pad. It was a mistake she made often. The sight of the third mat at the table somehow made her feel as if her mother were still with them.

"Oh, I know that one!" she heard her father say into the phone. "It's an elephant with wrinkled panty hose!"

"Is it Stevie?" Carole asked. The colonel nodded. Carole shook her head. Stevie was *her* best friend, but you'd never know it by the way Stevie and her father chatted on the phone. Both of them loved old corny jokes, and once they got started, there was no stopping them. Carole lowered the heat on the beef filling and began chopping lettuce.

"All right. So what's green and goes slam! slam! slam! slam!" There was a brief silence. "Give up? It's a four-door pickle!" Colonel Hanson chortled.

That was as much as Carole could take. Besides, she nearly sliced her finger as well as the lettuce. "My turn," she announced, wresting the phone from her father. He relinquished it gracefully and took over the chopping. "What's up?" Carole asked. She wrapped a paper towel around a small cut.

"I can't believe it, but both my parents are coming! I could just about kill my brothers—in fact I may still do it—but at least my parents will be at the meeting. They can sit with your dad."

"I don't know about that," Carole said. "I still haven't convinced him to come."

"Listen," Stevie said, "if I could talk my parents into it, you can *definitely* talk your dad into it."

"I just wish I knew what 'it' was," Carole said.

"Whatever 'it' is, it's important," Stevie said. "So go for it!"

"You have the most amazing way of seeing everything as a contest," Carole observed. "Like everything can be solved by winning one for the Gipper."

"Not everything," Stevie conceded.

"Such as?"

"Well, not science projects," she reminded Carole.

"True. Listen, I have to finish getting dinner together," Carole said. "Talk to you tomorrow."

Stevie wished her good luck and they hung up.

"What was that about?" Colonel Hanson asked.

Carole decided to let Stevie be an inspiration to her. "Oh, she was mostly calling to tell me how excited her parents are about going to the Pine Hollow meeting next Tuesday, and how glad they are to take time out of their busy lives to do something with their daughter, since it's something that matters a lot to her. Sure, it's a sacrifice. I mean, her father has to skip the annual Lawyer of the Year dinner, and he was supposed to receive the award, and her mother was scheduled to present a case to the Supreme Court the same day, but she told the justices they'll have to reschedule. It's a good thing they've got such flexible schedules, and nothing as critical as Navy-Bean Soup Night at the O-Club. Dinner's ready."

Carole filled the taco shells, served the rice and beans, and handed her father a dish.

"Pretty important, huh?" Colonel Hanson asked Carole while he sprinkled his tacos with cheese and olives.

"To me it is, Dad," Carole said. "I mean I really don't know what it's about, but it has to do with riding, and anything that has to do with riding is important. Can you come? Please?"

"Tell you what," he said. "I'll come to your meeting and then you and I can have dinner afterward at the Officers' Club."

"Gee, what an interesting idea," Carole said, pleased with his solution. It meant she'd have to wear a skirt to the meeting to be dressed properly for the O-Club dining room, but more importantly, it meant her father would be there. She felt giddy. "Do you suppose they'll be serving anything special that night?"

Her father grinned. Carole wondered if he'd known from the beginning that he would come. It didn't matter. He'd be there.

LISA WAS WORKING on algebra in the study hall when the door to the room opened. She didn't even notice.

X squared times X cubed equals X to the fifth, plus Y cubed times 7 times Y to the eighth power equals—she chomped on her eraser. It tasted terrible and didn't help at all.

"Lisa Atwood?" the study-hall monitor called. Lisa looked up. "There's a message for you." The monitor brought her the note. She didn't think she'd ever gotten a message in the middle of a study hall before—or in the middle of anything, for that matter. It made her a little nervous.

"Please meet your parents in front of the school at the end of the day," the note read. It was signed by the vice-principal of her school.

Lisa stared at the note, reading it again several times. The message didn't become any clearer on re-reading. Why on earth would her parents come to the school to pick her up? Their house was only a few blocks from school, a short walk that Lisa did by herself two times a day.

She remembered when one of her classmates had gotten a note like this. Her mother had been very ill. Perhaps one of Lisa's grandparents was ill? They'd all been very healthy when the family had visited them over the recent holiday weekend. But even if something had happened to one of them, why would her parents pick her up at school? It didn't make sense.

Lisa was a very logical person. It was one of the characteristics that helped her be an A-student. She applied all her logic to the situation, but nothing suggested itself as the answer. Logic wasn't going to work, she realized. She decided to return to algebra.

Y^3 *times* $7Y^8$ . . .

"Why would anybody want to multiply Y times itself three times, then multiply that by 7 and *that* times Y times itself eight times?" she asked herself. It was clear logic wasn't going to help her on that one either.

The bell rang. Lisa folded the note, put it into her algebra book, and headed for her history class.

"Hey, Lisa, is something wrong?" It was Carole. Although the two girls went to the same school, Carole was in the grade below Lisa and they rarely saw each other. If ever there had been a time when Lisa wanted to talk to Carole, this was it, but she had only three minutes between classes.

"Something's up with my parents," she explained quickly as they walked toward their next classes. "They're picking me up after school, but I don't know why. I'll call you tonight, if I can."

The look of concern on Carole's face was unmistakable. Lisa realized Carole probably had gotten notes at school about her mother.

"It's probably nothing to worry about," Lisa said. "After all, the note said they'd both be here."

"Oh, yeah, right," Carole said. "Well, call me tonight." She waved and headed for her English class.

Lisa was glad she'd been able to make Carole feel better. She just wished she could do the same for herself. Who could concentrate on the Wars of the Roses when she had gotten a note from the vice-principal? She felt in her pocket. It was still there. It was real.

The rest of the day was almost a total loss for her. She got three wrong answers on her history quiz and ended up telling her algebra teacher she didn't care what Y^3 times $7Y^8$ was, surprising both of them with that announcement. Usually Lisa cared very much about Y cubed.

At last the final bell rang. Lisa didn't even stop to think about what books she needed to take home. She grabbed all of them out of her locker and dashed for the front door of the school.

Both of her parents were standing at the curb, looking healthy and happy. What was going on?

"Oh, darling, we have such a wonderful surprise for you!" Mrs. Atwood announced, barely glancing at the colossal stack of books Lisa was carrying. Her father opened the trunk and Lisa dumped her lockerful of books into it. Then he opened the rear door of the car for her. Lisa slid into the backseat.

"Wonderful?" Lisa asked. "Tell me. I've been worried sick ever since I got your note!"

"We thought you might be," Mrs. Atwood said. "It was sort of a little joke."

What kind of a little joke was that? Suddenly Lisa didn't care what their wonderful news was. She was annoyed with their sense of humor.

"Well, aren't you going to ask?" her mother demanded as they pulled the doors shut on the car. "Don't bother, I can't wait to tell you. Your father and I have decided to buy you a horse! When I learned that the diAngelos were buying a new horse for Veronica, it just made sense that you should have one, too. So I spoke with Veronica's mother and she mentioned a horse she'd heard about."

Lisa wondered if she'd heard the words right. A horse? Her parents were going to buy *her* a horse of her own?

Her father started the car and drove them away from the school. Lisa hardly noticed. She was thinking about a horse—*her* horse. She could see it in her mind's eye. He was a sleek gray, tall, with slender but strong legs. His name was Silver. She'd whistle for him in the mornings and he'd come galloping across the paddock, nuzzle her shoulder, and stand still while she slid onto him, bareback.

She could almost feel the dewy grass tickle the bottoms of her bare feet and brush against her legs, the wind on her face, and the strength of the animal beneath her. Her horse—her very own horse.

Lisa sighed.

"Is something wrong, dear?" her mother asked.

"Oh, no. Everything's great. Really great. Tell me again about the horse we're seeing."

Mrs. Atwood fished a slip of paper out of her purse and read from it. "It's a gray mare named Streamline. She's belonged to this farm all her life and she's supposed to be very gentle. That's what the lady kept telling me on the phone."

Lisa had learned a few things about horses in the time she'd been riding. A horse that one person found gentle, another might find uncontrollable. She decided to reserve judgment about the animal until she was actually on her back. Still, she had a feeling that a horse named Streamline had to be wonderful.

Mr. Atwood turned into a drive marked by a hand-painted sign that read Horse for Sale. Lisa could feel her pulse quicken. As soon as the car pulled to a stop, she was out of the door. She waited impatiently while her mother knocked on the farmhouse door, and barely noticed as her parents introduced themselves and chatted with the owner. When the owner, Mrs.

Brandon, led them to the paddock, Lisa could hardly speak. She stared excitedly, waiting for Streamline to appear when Mrs. Brandon called her.

Nothing. There was no sign of Streamline.

"She usually likes to graze on the other side of the hill, where there's a little stream. Want to walk down there?"

Mrs. Atwood looked dubiously at the muddy ground and her suede pumps. She and Mr. Atwood decided to wait by the barn. Lisa and Mrs. Brandon would walk across the paddock.

Mrs. Brandon gave Lisa some carrots for the horse, and they started across the field. Mrs. Brandon led the way.

"She's a real sweet horse," Mrs. Brandon said, repeating her earlier statements. Lisa felt a little uneasy. Of course she wanted a sweet horse; she didn't want a wild, uncontrollable animal. But it seemed that all anybody could say about this horse was how sweet and gentle it was. There was a limit to sweetness, even in a horse.

Mrs. Brandon whistled. "Streamline!" she called. "We've got some juicy carrots for you!"

Nothing.

At last, Lisa and Mrs. Brandon reached the top of the hill and there, just as Mrs. Brandon had predicted, was Streamline. She was a big, tall gray horse whose coat had whitened with age. Lisa stopped and watched her while Mrs. Brandon approached. The horse didn't move. She continued munching contentedly on the sparse grass in the muddy paddock. When Mrs. Brandon clipped a lead rope on her, she obediently stopped munching and followed her owner.

"She's a good horse for a young rider, you know," Mrs. Brandon said when she and the horse reached Lisa. "Very gentle and sweet."

"Can I ride her?" Lisa asked.

"Of course. Her saddle's in the barn. Would you like to lead her?"

"Yes, but can I ride her now, I mean bareback?" Perhaps it was silly of her, but Lisa still had that picture in her mind of riding her own horse bareback in the early morning. It was something she'd done when she'd been at a dude ranch belonging to Kate Devine, an out-of-state Saddle Club member. They had all gone for a bareback ride at sunrise with their new friend, Christine Lonetree. To Lisa, it was part of what having her own horse would be like.

Mrs. Brandon shrugged. "Suit yourself," she said. "The horse is gentle enough."

Mrs. Brandon gave Lisa a lift onto the horse. Lisa thought it might not have been necessary. She was beginning to suspect that Streamline was so gentle that she could have hauled herself up by the horse's tail and Streamline wouldn't have protested. And that was a problem. This horse seemed to have no spirit to speak of.

Lisa nudged Streamline with her heels and the horse

began walking on signal. It was a smooth gait, but most walks were.

"Can I take her to a trot?" Lisa asked.

"If you can stay on," Mrs. Brandon said, handing Lisa the lead rope.

Lisa kicked again. Streamline kept on walking placidly. It took another half dozen kicks before Streamline was trotting, and that lasted only a few steps before the horse resumed walking again. Lisa tried clicking her tongue and slapping the mare's flanks with her hand, but it didn't inspire Streamline. Lisa began to wonder how a horse whose best gait—perhaps only gait—was a walk, got the name Streamline. She didn't want a wild horse she'd be worrying about all the time, but she did want a horse with some independence.

"We've been using her for rides with the children around here," Mrs. Brandon said. "Wouldn't hurt a fly, you know."

"I can tell," Lisa said.

"Anybody's real safe on this horse," Mrs. Brandon said.

"I'm sure they would be," Lisa told her. Mrs. Brandon looked pleased. Streamline must have been a wonderful horse for the Brandons—just what they'd needed. Mrs. Brandon appeared to be glad that Lisa could appreciate the horse's strong points.

"Everybody likes Streamline. You do, too, don't you?" Mrs. Brandon asked.

Lisa nodded. Of course she liked Streamline. How could anybody not like her? The problem was that Lisa didn't want to *own* Streamline. She didn't know how to explain this to her parents without hurting Mrs. Brandon's feelings.

Lisa's parents were waiting for them expectantly at the paddock gate. "Do you love her?" her mother asked.

Lisa felt uncomfortable with the question, but she knew what her answer was going to be. "She's a really sweet horse," Lisa began tactfully.

Mrs. Brandon interrupted before Lisa could continue. "Sure your daughter loves Streamline," she said. "Everybody loves Streamline, but she's not the right horse for Lisa and I'm not going to sell her to you."

Mr. Atwood was astonished. "What are you talking about? You said the horse was for sale. We can pay your price. Don't you want the money?"

Mrs. Brandon tied Streamline's lead rope to the fence and helped Lisa dismount. "Money isn't the issue here. Your daughter and my horse are the issues. Your daughter's a good rider and she's going to be a better rider. Streamline's a good horse for bad riders, but a bad horse for good riders. She's safe and gentle, but Lisa's already outgrown Streamline's temperament and she'll want a different horse within a year. That's not fair to either of them. Streamline belongs with a family with a lot of little kids who will use her as a first horse, where she'll get loads of love. And Lisa deserves a horse she can grow with."

Lisa patted Streamline and gave her a carrot.

"How do you feel about this, dear?" Mrs. Atwood asked.

"I couldn't have said it better myself." She climbed over the paddock fence and, while her mother scraped the mud off her shoes, Lisa got the names of a couple of other places where she might find a horse for herself.

"Good luck!" Mrs. Brandon called. Lisa and her parents waved good-bye. Streamline just munched contentedly on the sparse grass.

IT TOOK LISA two trips to get all of her books out of the trunk of the car. She wondered, as she carried the second load up to her room, how she'd managed to get them all out there in one trip in the first place. It must have been adrenaline, she decided.

She was still full of adrenaline, too. She had some absolutely wonderful news to share with her friends. Even though Streamline wasn't the horse for her, her parents weren't giving up. They were serious about buying her a horse, her very own horse. She could hardly wait to tell Carole and Stevie. She raced up the stairs with her second load of books and headed for the phone on her bedside table.

Stevie's line was busy. Stevie's line was always busy. Even when Stevie's parents had given up and gotten a separate line for Stevie and her brothers, the problem hadn't been solved. In fact, Stevie and her brothers seemed to spend *more* time on the phone. Lisa thought about pretending that she'd forgotten Stevie's number and calling on the parents' line, but she didn't think the Lakes would believe her.

She decided to call Carole instead. The phone rang three times before Carole answered it, out of breath.

"Hi, Carole, it's me, Lisa. Did you have to run for the phone?"

"No, I mean, yes. Well, sort of. See, I just got home from Pine Hollow and I was in front of the house, so I heard the phone ringing and I had to run a bit. No trouble. Let me just get my book bag off." There was a pause and Lisa heard a loud thunk. "I had to call you anyway, so I'm glad you called."

Carole's tone of voice made Lisa realize that her own good news was going to have to wait until her friend had told her what was bothering her.

"What's up?" Lisa asked.

"Oh, it's Veronica. You won't believe it. She's got her new horse *already!*" Carole had been there when the van had arrived, and she told Lisa all about it.

"That horse just about prances instead of walking. And what a face!"

Arabians were famous for having pretty heads and faces, and Garnet, it seemed, was no exception. Garnet was being stabled in the stall that had belonged to Cobalt. Cobalt's death had hurt Carole deeply, and the more Carole talked, the more Lisa realized that her friend was afraid that Veronica's carelessness was going to hurt her new horse as well.

". . . and she just yanked at the lead rope when the horse was coming out of the van! That's no way to unload a horse. You *lead* them, you don't yank them. You know that. I know that. Everybody but Veronica knows that! So why is it that Veronica's the one with the new horse?"

"You know as well as I do," Lisa said, but Carole didn't respond to her comment.

"Then, the horse hadn't even been out of the van and on hard ground for thirty seconds when Veronica was looking around for somebody to help her! That girl doesn't know the first thing about horses! Owning a horse is really a lot more responsibility than it is fun—though I'd gladly take on the responsibility. Anyway, for me, *anything* to do with horses is fun. I'd even enjoy mucking out the stall for my own horse. But nobody who isn't willing to do the work should take on the job. And Veronica thinks cleaning a *water bucket* is beneath her. Believe me, she shouldn't take on the job of owning a horse. She's just not fit to own one. You should have seen the business of the blanket!"

Lisa listened while Carole described Veronica's unwillingness to put a blanket on Garnet, even though there was a chill in the stable. Mrs. Reg, Max's mother, who helped her son run the stables, had loaned Veronica a blanket for the horse, but Veronica was upset because she didn't like the color of the blanket. Lisa knew that everything Carole was saying was true, and that Veronica was really very unfit to own Garnet, just as she'd been unfit to own Cobalt. She hadn't learned a thing from Cobalt's tragic death. But Lisa felt there was more to what Carole was saying than that.

Lisa knew Carole well enough to know that horses were her life, not just a fashionable hobby, as they were for Veronica. What Carole wanted more than anything was to own a horse. It was something she dreamed about every single night, and Lisa thought that underneath all the anger, her friend was very jealous.

It would not have crossed Carole's mind to be envious of Veronica's designer clothes, her big house, her own VCR, her gigantic swimming pool, or her vacations in Europe. None of that meant anything to Carole. What meant something to Carole was horses. Veronica had one, Carole did not. And that was something to envy.

It suddenly occurred to Lisa that Carole might be jealous of her, too, if she had a horse. The thought upset her, and she couldn't quite bring herself to tell Carole about her parents' decision. She didn't even want to tell her about Streamline and the wise owner who didn't want Lisa to buy her.

"So, guess who got to groom Garnet?" Carole continued, not noticing her friend's silence. "You got it. I groomed her. You won't believe how silky her coat is. It's very soft and it gleams when you groom it just right. After I was all done, Veronica's parents came in and admired the horse—not the job I'd done, of course—the *horse*. They are just as awful as *she* is! By the way, speaking of parents, what was up with yours this afternoon?"

Carole could talk about horses by the hour, but eventually, she would remember other things, too. Lisa had been hoping that Carole would forget about the note and how upset she'd been in school. But Carole was a good friend. She cared too much to let those things slip for long.

"My parents?" Lisa said, stalling for time.

"Yeah, the note they sent you—that they were picking you up. What was that all about?"

"Oh, that. It turned out to be nothing at all. They were together and knew they'd be near school when it let out, so they just picked me up and drove me home." The explanation sounded lame, but Lisa hoped it would work.

"Oh," Carole said. "I'm glad everything's okay. I've got to go now. I'm going to make a list of gear that Veronica will have to get for Garnet. She'll never do it without my help, you know, and a horse really ought to have its own grooming gear—especially a horse as good as Garnet. Bye. See you in riding class tomorrow, and then at Max's big meeting! Any more ideas what it's about?"

"No brainstorm yet. Bye-bye."

Lisa hung up the phone. She felt terrible about keeping the truth from Carole. What was the right thing to do? She was too confused to figure it out herself; she needed help.

One thing she'd learned over the last few months was that she could always get help from The Saddle Club. Obviously she couldn't talk to Carole, but she could discuss the problem with Stevie and possibly come up with a solution.

Lisa reached for the phone again, but then she had a better idea. Stevie was expecting her to come over and help with the science project this evening anyway, so it could wait until after dinner. She'd go to Stevie's house and tell her about it, in person. Stevie would know what to do. Stevie always had the answer.

"WAIT A MINUTE," Lisa told Stevie as she stared at the confused array of seeds, pots, and dirt better known as Stevie's science project. "You have to be logical. Now, let's think this through. Your project is to show how important water and light are to seed germination. So you set up one pot with seeds that get both light and water, one that gets light but not water, and one that gets water but not light. Oh, yes, and one that doesn't get either. That's very important. That's your control."

"That's it?" Stevie asked.

"Yeah, that's it," Lisa said. "And it turns out that you need both light and water—big surprise—to get the seeds to grow. It'll take about ten days to get con-clusive results. Don't forget which pots need water, okay?"

Stevie nodded sheepishly. It always seemed simple once somebody helped her sort out what was impor-tant from what wasn't. She was very glad Lisa had come to help her. As she began putting soil in the pots, she told her so.

"Thanks a lot. I probably would have figured it out eventually, but you saved me a whole lot of trouble. When I couldn't reach you this afternoon, I was going to call Carole, but she was so upset about Garnet—did she tell you?"

"Yeah, she did," Lisa said. "And that reminds me of what I wanted to tell you about—"

"You should have seen Veronica this afternoon," Stevie interrupted. She really wanted to tell Lisa what it had been like. "She out-Veronica-ed Veronica! That horse wasn't out of the van two seconds before she was looking around for somebody else to do her work for her! Of course, Carole pitched right in. When there's a job to be done and it has to do with horses, it's Carole to the rescue. Veronica's unbelievable! And the really insane part was that her parents were right there and they didn't even seem to notice that Veronica was totally useless!"

Each of the four pots in front of Stevie was now two-thirds filled with soil. Stevie opened the seed pouch. She'd chosen radishes because they grew so fast. She dumped one quarter of the packet in each of the four pots.

"Stevie! You don't need to put so many seeds in!" Lisa said.

"This way at least something will grow," Stevie reasoned.

"And you may have to change your experiment to whether plants need any room in the pot to grow!"

Reluctantly, Stevie fished the extra seeds out of each pot and then covered the remaining ones with another half inch of soil. She patted the soil down gently, dusted off her hands, and began to write the labels. When she finished, she noticed the labels were smeared with dirt. She stuck them on the pots regardless. Stevie figured it didn't matter much. The pots were dirty anyway. Growing things was a dirty business.

"So anyway," Stevie continued, anxious to finish telling Lisa about Veronica, "Carole groomed Garnet and I got her feed ready. Veronica stood there with her hands on her hips, like a queen overseeing her servants. Honestly, that girl has no business owning a horse! The worst of it is, she's got one, and I don't!" It didn't seem fair to Stevie. A horse was something to be earned!

She poured water into two of the pots and then realized that Lisa was being strangely silent.

"Is something wrong?" she asked Lisa. "I mean,

other than the obvious fact that Veronica doesn't deserve Garnet?"

"Oh, no," Lisa said. "It's just that—uh, well, I'm
sorry I missed seeing Garnet today. I guess she's a real
beauty."

"She is," Stevie assured Lisa. "But don't worry.
You'll have plenty of opportunities to see Garnet, and
groom Garnet, and feed Garnet, and clean Garnet's
tack. You just won't have a chance to ride Garnet.
That privilege will be saved for the queen herself. Now
help me find a space in my closet for the pots that
don't get any light, will you?"

THAT NIGHT, LISA lay in her bed, her head swimming
with confused thoughts. Something was terribly
wrong, and she needed to understand it. As she had
done with Stevie's science project, she tried to sort the
facts into logical order.

She had some good news, really good news, but if
she told the two people she most wanted to tell, she
might hurt them. It wasn't as if it were good news that
she could hide. After all, a horse was too big to hide
for very long. Then her friends would be angry at her
for not telling, *and* jealous of her as well.

Because it was jealousy that made them so angry at
Veronica, wasn't it?

5

CAROLE WAS HAVING a difficult time concentrating on her riding class. She found herself looking at the door almost every minute. She was waiting for her father. He'd said he would be there and she knew she could count on him. She wasn't worried that he wouldn't show up, she was just anxious that he was coming. She was also more than a little anxious to know what the meeting after class was all about.

"Now I want you all to canter without stirrups," Max announced. "This is a balance exercise for you. Cross your stirrups up over your saddle and . . . begin!"

Carole followed his instructions, as she always did, but her eyes remained on the doorway. It confused her horse. One of the first things a rider learns is to look in the direction she wants her horse to go. Horses seem to sense that, perhaps from a shift in balance. Not looking in the right direction is one of the easiest ways to lose points in a competition.

"Eyes forward!" Max warned her. He didn't have to say it again, though, because just then Colonel Hanson arrived. Carole grinned at him and then completely turned her attention to her riding.

Soon after her father sat down on one of the benches around the ring, other parents started arriving. Within a short time, parents were waving at riders, riders were waving at parents, and Max was totally frustrated.

"Okay, I guess it's time to call it quits," he told his students. "I want you to dismount and walk your horses until they've cooled down. Then untack them, water and feed them, and our meeting will begin."

Carole slid down out of the saddle. Her father walked over to her and tentatively patted her horse, Barq.

"Why do you have to walk him?" he asked.

Carole explained that if you put a horse in his stall before he had a chance to walk and cool down, he could stiffen up and have some bad muscle problems, and sometimes complicated digestive problems.

"Oh," the colonel said, holding the reins while Carole loosened Barq's girth for his cooling walk.

Carole was surprised, during the next half hour, at how much she had to tell her father. She had been around horses and loved them all her life. He had always supported her love of horses, and she had always assumed that he knew as much as she did. But, she realized, he really didn't know much about them. He didn't even know how to lead a horse!

Finally, the work was finished. Barq and the other horses were cooled, groomed, bedded, and fed. The riders had changed into their street clothes. It was time for the meeting to begin. All the young riders and their parents gathered in the spacious living room of Max's house, which adjoined Pine Hollow Stables.

"I've asked you all to come," Max began, "because I want to talk to you about an exciting new opportunity for my young riders and their parents. I have just received a letter from the U.S. Pony Clubs, approving my application to begin our own club at Pine Hollow."

Carole couldn't contain her gasp. Their own Pony Club! Max smiled while the others looked at her in surprise. Carole could tell that she and Max were the only ones who really knew what that would mean. She listened excitedly while Max explained it to the others. Pony Clubs were local groups, part of a national organization that sponsored instruction and activities for young riders.

There were usually weekly meetings for each local club and then monthly or seasonal "rallies" where several nearby clubs could get together and have competition and instruction periods.

Pony Clubs also had their own rating systems for members, based on the completion of specific tasks and goals. They weren't just things you could learn from books, either. Every Pony Club member was expected to learn not only about riding, but also about horse care, stable management, and even veterinary care. Pony Clubs really covered just about everything having to do with horses.

"One of the most important factors in having our own Pony Club," Max continued, "actually, the one essential thing, is parent support. Unless we have a minimum of parents from five families, we won't be able to have our club. It would be a big time commitment, I know, but I can promise you that if your son or daughter cares about horses, the time you invest in our Pony Club will be well worth it. Has anybody here ever been in a Pony Club before?" Max asked.

Carole raised her hand. Once, when her father was stationed at a large base in California, there was a Pony Club on the base. At that time, Carole's father had been doing a lot of traveling, so he hadn't been able to be involved at all. Now that she knew how little he knew about horses, Carole didn't think that was so bad.

She told the other riders how much she'd liked the Pony Club and how much she'd learned. "One of the neatest things about it was that you learn so much about everything—and you're tested on it, too. You may be the best rider in the stables, but if you don't know how to mix bran mash for your horse, you're a D-1 with the eight-year-olds." Carole couldn't help smiling to herself. She had the funniest feeling that the arrival of Garnet might have had something to do with Max's interest in a Pony Club for Pine Hollow. Something good was going to come out of Veronica's incompetence after all!

During the next forty-five minutes, Max gave everybody booklets from the USPC, handed out copies of *The Manual of Horsemanship*, explaining that it was the Pony Clubbers' bible, and answered what seemed like hundreds of questions.

One of the parents asked if everybody had to have his own horse to join the Pony Club.

"Not at all," Max said. "The fact is that most Pony Clubbers do have their own horses, but it's not a requirement. Very few of the riders here own their own horses, but they're all eligible for membership. Pine Hollow will permit the use of its horses for approved Pony Club activities. Pony Clubs are good for riders, but they're good for riding, too."

"Will you do all the instruction?" another parent asked.

"No, though I'll usually be part of the meetings. Instruction will come from other experts. Judy Barker, my vet, has agreed to help. Also, the children will learn from other local professionals, the farrier, the saddlery, the grain-and-feed place. But mostly, the riders will learn from you, their parents, and from themselves. Which brings me back to where I began. You parents are a critical part of this. The club needs your help. Do I have any volunteers?"

There was silence in the room. Carole, who was sitting on the floor near Max between Stevie and Lisa, turned to look. All they needed were five hands to go up, five family volunteers who would make the difference between Pony Club and no Pony Club.

Nobody moved. Carole crossed her fingers.

Meg Durham's mother raised her hand.

"Thank you," Max said.

Carole crossed her legs.

Betsy Cavanaugh's father and mother both raised their hands.

"Thank you," Max said.

Carole crossed her arms across her crossed legs.

A pair of parents she didn't even know raised their hands. Another mother raised her hand.

"Thank you," Max said.

Carole crossed her eyes.

Colonel Hanson raised his hand.

"That's it, that's five!" Max announced. "We can have a Pony Club!"

Dad? What is he doing raising his hand? He doesn't know the first thing about horses. He doesn't even know how to lead them! Carole could hardly keep from staring at her father. He beamed back at her proudly. Carole shrugged to herself. What did it matter, anyway? Most of the other parents knew a lot about horses. The only reason her father needed to raise his hand was to keep Max and the USPC happy.

"Now our next order of business is to come up with a name for our club," Max said. "A lot of times, the clubs are named after the towns or the stables they're in. We could call this Willow Creek Pony Club or Pine Hollow, if you like. As far as I know, though, there's no limitation. This is our club and we can call it anything we like, but I do have to put a name on the final application. Any suggestions?" Max paused, but no one spoke. "I'll tell you what," Max continued. "We'll take a little break now. My mother has set out some cold drinks and we can talk about a name when we reconvene in about ten minutes."

"I have a suggestion," came Veronica's unmistakable voice.

"Yes?" Max said.

"Why don't we call it The Saddle Club?"

There were three gasps in the room at once. Carole knew just where the other two had come from. This was Veronica's revenge for being excluded from their club.

"Not bad," Max said. Carole realized he'd seen the

looks of concern on the girls' faces and was stalling for them. "Let's have our break now," he said. "We'll take other suggestions and then vote."

Carole, Lisa, and Stevie looked at one another and nodded. They knew what had to be done. It was time for an emergency Saddle Club meeting. They gathered in an isolated corner of the room, far away from the apple cider and homemade cookies.

"We've just got to vote it down, that's all," Lisa said. "I mean, The Saddle Club is *our* name. It's special and it's not something I want to share with Veronica. She just wants to steal our name."

"I don't think so," Stevie said. "I think she just wants to know what The Saddle Club is. She's forcing our hand so we'll have to tell everybody. Frankly, I don't mind telling anybody about The Saddle Club, but I do mind being forced into it by Veronica."

"Same here," Carole said. "But it's a terrific name. How do we get it voted down?"

"Simple," Stevie replied. "We come up with something better!"

"But what could be better?" Lisa asked. "The Saddle Club is a just about perfect name!"

"For us it is," Carole said. "But when you think about it, it's not really what Pony Clubs are about. Pony Clubs are about learning about horses, not just riding. It wises you up on subjects like stable management and horse care, safety, training. The whole idea is to teach everything. The qualifications aren't just to be horse crazy, like our club, but to learn all the whys and wherefores of horses."

"That's it!" Stevie interrupted her. Carole and Lisa looked at her in surprise. "You said it," she told Carole.

"Me? What did I say?"

"You said it twice, in fact. You said this club will wise us up and teach us all the whys of horses. The proper name of the club, therefore, is Horse Wise." Stevie smiled beatifically, and folded her hands on her lap.

Lisa and Carole, laughing, had to agree. The Saddle Club meeting was over. It was time to return to Max's meeting. They took the last three glasses of cider and returned to their places near Max.

When Max asked for other suggestions, Carole raised her hand. She stood up and explained what she knew about Pony Clubs, stressing the idea of how they made riders *wise* and didn't just teach them about riding, as the name Saddle Club might suggest. She tried to sound very polite to Veronica, but she knew Veronica knew she wasn't being polite. She used every bit of debating skill she had to convince people to vote on their name. Only four people in the room really knew what was going on. It didn't matter, though. The fact was, Carole was winning and she knew it.

". . . so, my friends and I would like to suggest that we name our club Horse Wise."

"Hey, great idea!" Max said, publicly casting his

vote. That was what they'd needed. By voice vote, their Pony Club got its own, unusual name.

Carole felt so good at the end of the meeting that she didn't even care when Veronica make a nasty remark on her way out. "Nice job, Carole," she snapped, "but it means that the first time you ride Garnet will be when it snows in July."

6

WHENEVER THE SUBJECT was horses, Carole was
happy. This evening, she was especially happy.
Even Veronica diAngelo hadn't been able to ruin it.
Pine Hollow was going to have its own Pony Club!

"We're having our first meeting next week," she
told her father as they headed for the car.

"I heard," he said. Carole thought maybe he was
teasing her a little bit, but she didn't mind.

"It's a mounted meeting, you know," she said as
she took her place in the front seat of the car, next
to her father.

"I heard, but what does that mean?" he asked.

"It means we'll be mounted—you know, on
horseback."

"Oh." Colonel Hanson started the car. "With
your saddles, right?"

"Sure we'll have saddles. If there weren't going to be saddles, we'd call it *bare*back."

"That makes sense," he said, pulling the car out of Pine Hollow's driveway. He turned the car toward the base, where the Officers' Club and navy-bean soup awaited them.

Carole couldn't stop talking about the Pony Club. "Then, at other times, we'll have unmounted meetings. I can't wait until the farrier talks to us. That should be neat."

"What's a farrier?" Colonel Hanson asked. "Someone who makes fair coats?"

"Very funny, but no," Carole said patiently. "A farrier is a blacksmith. He makes horseshoes and fits them properly to the horse's hooves and nails them on."

"Nails them? Doesn't that hurt?"

"No, the horse's hoof is like a toenail. As long as the nail just goes into the toenail part, the horse can't even feel it."

"You mean there are other parts to the foot?" her father asked.

"Oh, sure, there's the frog and the bulbs and the sole and that's just the beginning. Horses' feet are very complicated."

"I guess they are," the colonel said. He was quiet for a while and seemed to be thinking. It gave Carole some time to think as well. Carole knew a lot about horses. She'd read a lot of books, but mostly she'd learned because she spent time with people who knew a lot about horses and who had taught her about them. That was one of the best things about a Pony Club. All the members were there to learn and all the volunteers were there to teach them.

But what about a volunteer who didn't know anything? One who didn't know the difference between horseback and bareback? What good was he going to be? There was something else bothering her, too, but she couldn't quite put her finger on it.

Her father began singing. He loved music from the fifties and sixties. He started in on an Elvis Presley medley, beginning with his favorite, "Big Boots."

Carole looked at him from the corner of her eye. Usually, she liked it when he sang or told his silly old jokes. Usually, she liked almost everything he did. But was she going to like it when he became part of her riding and showed everybody that he didn't know anything?

Carole was very proud of her skill in riding and her knowledge. She loved it when people asked her questions and she knew the answer. She knew she had a tendency to give them more answer than they might want. It was something her friends liked to tease her about, but she didn't mind. She still liked just plain knowing.

So now, how were people going to feel about her when they saw that her father, her wonderful father who could do so many other things, was a total ignoramus when it came to horses? And how was that going to make Carole feel?

"Dad?" she said, interrupting "Heartbreak Hotel."

"What, honey?"

"I have a couple of books you might want to look at about horses," she said.

"That's okay, sweetheart," he said. "I'm sure that whatever I need to know, you can tell me."

Carole sighed. That was what she was afraid of.

AFTER THE MEETING, Lisa's parents were more enthusiastic than ever about buying a horse for her. Lisa suspected it was because they had seen how few of the riders there actually did own their horses. She didn't think that was a very good reason for buying a horse, certainly no better than buying one because Veronica diAngelo had one. Still, she herself wanted to own one very much, and as long as her parents wanted to buy a horse, she didn't really care why.

The very next day, they picked her up after school again. The secretary from the vice-principal's office had given Lisa a strange look when she'd given her the second note about meeting her parents after school in less than a week, but that was another thing Lisa decided not to worry about.

This time, the farm was really a horse farm, not just a farm with a horse for sale. Lisa liked the place immediately. It had big, airy, light stalls for its horses. They all opened onto individual outdoor paddock areas.

Those areas, in turn, opened to a large field. The horses had plenty of room to move, but their movements were controlled. The place seemed like a good combination of stabling and pasturing.

The owner, Mr. Jenrette, greeted the Atwoods. He explained that he'd just acquired a horse, Brinker, as part of a package deal, but he wasn't a breeding horse so Mr. Jenrette wanted to sell him right away.

"He's a real beauty," Mr. Jenrette said. "I know you'll love him. I've already had three other phone calls about him. You're lucky that you called first." Mr. Jenrette led them over to the paddock. Brinker was a bay, which meant he was brown with a black mane and tail. Brinker's nose and ankles were black as well— that was called having black points—and he had a white blaze on his forehead.

Brinker was in his paddock. Lisa approached him slowly. He looked up and walked over toward her. It was as if they were already friends. The horse gazed at her curiously, and she patted his forehead. He seemed to like it, so she did it some more. Then she patted his neck.

"Here are some carrots," Mr. Jenrette said, offering her a handful. Lisa took one and gave it to Brinker. She loved the sound of a horse crunching on carrots. Brinker loved the carrot.

"He's not a purebred or anything," Mr. Jenrette said. "But he's got good lines. You'll love riding him for a long time to come."

"What does that mean?" Mrs. Atwood asked. Lisa explained that calling a horse purebred meant that it was registered as part of a breed, such as Thoroughbred, Arabian, or Quarter Horse. Both of its parents had to be registered and had to have the papers to prove it. It was a guarantee of quality breeding, though not necessarily of a good horse, and it was a guarantee of cost.

"You know something about horses, don't you?" Mr. Jenrette asked.

"A bit," Lisa said. "And I read a lot, too."

"I can tell," he said. Then he turned to her parents. "So, do you want him?" he asked.

"Oh, I think so," Mr. Atwood said, and he turned to Lisa for confirmation. "Is this the right one?" he asked.

"He certainly looks good," she said. "And I think I like his disposition—at least his stable manners. But there are lots of things we have to check first."

"Like what?" her mother asked. "The horse is pretty, you like him, he's for sale. What else is there?" Mrs. Atwood turned to Mr. Jenrette for an answer. The answer he gave was to look at his watch, as if he were waiting for the next buyer to show up and make him a better offer. It was a small gesture, but it told Lisa a lot. Lisa had a few doubts, and that little gesture gave her the confidence to follow up on them. Mr. Jenrette seemed to be very anxious to sell his horse.

"I need to check a few things," she said, climbing over the fence into the paddock. It made her even more suspicious that Mr. Jenrette didn't join her and help her. She wanted to check the horse's conformation, to make sure he had no obvious physical defects. She was no expert, so she could have used some expert advice. Why didn't Mr. Jenrette want to give it to her?

An expert could determine a lot of things by looking at a horse. There were many small things that could be wrong that might not mean much at the time of a purchase, but could cost thousands of dollars in veterinary bills over time. There were also lots of things that could seem odd, but not mean anything at all. So why didn't Mr. Jenrette want to show Lisa how good Brinker's conformation was?

Her parents watched, confused, while she checked the points she could. Mr. Jenrette just kept looking at his watch whenever he thought somebody was looking at him. Lisa definitely smelled a rat. Now, instead of being doubtful, she was sure there was something significantly wrong with the horse, and it became a challenge to her. Would she find it before Mr. Jenrette sprained his wrist looking at his watch?

It was almost like a game of Hot and Cold. When Lisa was looking at Brinker's head and neck, his body and his flanks, Mr. Jenrette had his hands on his hips. As soon as she picked up a hoof to examine Brinker's foot, Mr. Jenrette began looking at his watch. She let go of the hoof and the man's hand went into his pocket. When she knelt to study the foot as it sat on the ground, he spoke.

"Did you hear a car come in the drive?" he asked. He wasn't being subtle at all.

The problem had to be in Brinker's feet and legs. Lisa thought she spotted it. There was a complex set of bones at what might be called the horse's ankle, leading up to the main lower-leg bone, the cannon. Lisa didn't know the names of all the parts, but she knew that the lowest portion of the leg was supposed to be at approximately the same angle as the hoof, almost as if it were a continuation of the hoof. That wasn't the case on Brinker. His leg went straight up right above the hoof.

"Hmmm," she said.

"Next people are coming in about five minutes," Mr. Jenrette said.

"I'd like to try riding him, and then we'll have our vet check him out tomorrow," Lisa told him.

"He'll be sold by then," Mr. Jenrette said.

That was when Lisa decided it didn't matter whether she was right or wrong about where the problem was. If Mr. Jenrette expected to sell the horse to somebody who would not have it checked by a vet, he was definitely hiding something a vet would find. Brinker was a pretty horse, and he seemed to have a sweet disposition. But Brinker was not a horse she was going to own.

"No, thank you," Lisa said.

Mr. Jenrette shrugged. "Your loss."

"What's going on here?" Mr. Atwood demanded, suddenly realizing he'd been missing out on an entire drama.

As confident as she was that something was wrong, Lisa didn't want to make a scene. She'd explain to her parents on the way home. She tried to think of a reason that would satisfy them.

"It's just that the color doesn't seem right to me, Dad. You know I've got my heart set on a chestnut," Lisa said. It was about the dumbest reason she could think of for deciding not to buy a horse, but maybe it would work.

"Oh," her father said.

"Sure," her mother said. "Those are the sort of auburn-colored ones, aren't they? I love that color. I'm sure we can find a horse like that for you, dear. I just didn't know—"

"It's okay, Mom, and thanks, Mr. Jenrette," Lisa said, shaking his hand vigorously. She had the wild idea of trying to give his right wrist as much exercise as his left wrist had been getting. It was all she could do to keep from laughing as she did it.

Once the Atwoods were on the road, Lisa's father looked at her in the rearview mirror. "A chestnut?" he asked. "What was that all about?" She'd fooled her mother, but not her father. She doubted that she'd fooled Mr. Jenrette, either.

"Well," Lisa began.

"It was the vet part, wasn't it?" Mr. Atwood asked.

"Yeah," Lisa said, smiling. "As soon as he didn't want a vet looking at the horse, I knew something was wrong—really wrong. I think Brinker has a problem with his hooves and legs, but a vet would know for sure."

"This horse-buying business is a complicated one, isn't it?" Mr. Atwood asked.

"Yes," Lisa agreed. "It is." They had found one horse that was sound, but not right for her. Another was right for her, but not sound. It was a complicated business, and it was even more complicated than her father realized, because he had no way of knowing how much Lisa wanted to tell her friends and how afraid she was of doing it.

"I'm going to be away on business for a couple of days," Mr. Atwood said. "We'll look at more horses when I get back, okay?"

Lisa nodded.

"Don't worry. We'll find you the right horse," he assured her.

Lisa nodded again. After all, that was what she wanted, wasn't it?

"HORSE WISE, COME to order!"

Stevie tugged ever so slightly on Topside's reins. The horse stood still, seeming to sense that something exciting was about to happen. And something exciting *was* about to happen. The first Horse Wise mounted meeting was about to begin. All of the riders were about to become full-fledged members of the Pony Club.

It took a few minutes for all the horses to line up, especially since Veronica was riding Garnet in a group for the first time. It wasn't that Veronica couldn't control Garnet; it was that she didn't want to control her. As long as Garnet was acting up, Veronica was the center of attention and almost everybody had to look at her and her beautiful horse. Stevie stared straight ahead, and so did Lisa and Carole. Finally, Garnet was in line with everybody else. Max gave Veronica a warning look that told her to keep it that way.

"Our agenda for today is as follows," Max began. "First, each of you will receive your official Pony Club pins. You are entitled to wear them as long as you are a member in good standing of Horse Wise."

Stevie decided she intended to be a member in good standing for a very long time.

"Next, we will discuss the schedule for future meetings as well as ratings, and then we will play a learning game. This will be followed by a short trail ride and then the meeting will adjourn one half hour before scheduled to allow you all ample time for grooming and horse care. Remember, stable management and horse care are an important part of Horse Wise and will be required of all members."

That was when all three of The Saddle Club girls looked at Veronica. She didn't look back.

Max asked the sponsors to distribute the pins. Colonel Hanson was the first one to help. He took the pins from Max and began handing them out, walking behind the Pony Clubbers' horses as he went. Everyone at the meeting, except Colonel Hanson, knew that whenever it is practical, it makes sense to walk in front of horses, rather than behind them. Horses like to know what is going on and can get skittish if somebody passes too close to them.

"Colonel," Max said. "It's better to walk in front of the horses than in back of them."

"Oh," the colonel said sheepishly, coming quickly to the front of the group.

"Can anybody tell the colonel the reason for this?" Max asked. Several hands went up. Max called on Stevie, who quickly explained it. She thought she'd done a pretty good job, but after she finished, she noticed that Carole was scowling a little bit. Stevie thought about it for a few seconds and realized that Carole probably wasn't scowling at her. Maybe she was scowling because her father didn't know such a simple thing about horses. Carole was usually so patient when people didn't know things, but of course it was different when it was your own father. Stevie suspected that Colonel Hanson would never make that mistake again.

Once all the riders had their pins on, Max announced his schedule for the next few weeks. As long as the weather was good, they would alternate mounted meetings one Saturday and unmounted meetings the next. The following week, Judy, the vet, would talk to them about horse care, and at the meeting after that, the members would be tested and rated.

Stevie had been reading up on Pony Clubs. And when Phil Marston had called her the other night, she'd asked him about them since he already belonged. In fact, their clubs were in the same district and they'd be seeing each other at rallies. Stevie could hardly wait. In the meantime, though, she'd have to be "rated." Each member would receive a rating according to his own skill level. The ratings started at D-1 through 3, which was for beginners, then progressed to C-1 through 3, B, H-A, and A. Very few riders ever achieved H-A and A and only very good riders, with years of experience, got to B. Stevie hoped that one day she'd be able to be a C, but for now, she figured that she and Lisa were both D's. Carole might make it to C. Stevie wondered what sort of rating they would come up with for Veronica. The important thing about the ratings, and about Pony Clubs in general, was that they weren't just about riding. Horse care was just as important. Stevie grinned. Veronica wouldn't be able to find a stableboy to take the horse-care section of the test for her!

"All right, now, our first activity will be a game called Giant Steps."

Max described the rules. Each rider would be asked a question about horses. If the rider answered correctly, his or her horse could take one step toward a line that Max had Colonel Hanson draw in the dirt. If the rider made a mistake, the horse would have to take a step backward toward another line. Whoever crossed the front line first, won. Whoever crossed the back line was out.

Max began shooting out questions. How many beats were in a walk? Trot? Canter?

Stevie thought they were very easy questions until she noticed that the riders he was giving them to were beginners. They weren't easy questions for them.

"Stevie, name the parts of a horse's neck."

Stevie made a face. Veronica diAngelo laughed. That was the inspiration Stevie needed.

"Poll, crest, and withers," she answered. She was awarded one giant step.

Carole named ten grooming aids, and Lisa told him five registered breeds of horses.

"Veronica, name three parts of the horse's foot."

Veronica shifted uncomfortably in her saddle. Stevie suddenly got the feeling she was going to like this a lot.

"Well, there's the hoof—"

"One step backward," Max announced. "Anybody else?"

Stevie raised her hand. Max called on her. "Wall, sole, and frog," she said. She stepped forward.

"Veronica, I told you to step backward," Max said.

Veronica glared at him. "Isn't it time to stop this game now and go for a trail ride?" she said.

"Not yet." That closed the subject for everybody except Veronica, who was never one to enjoy public humiliation.

Garnet started acting up a little, as if she didn't want to step backward any more than Veronica did. Stepping backward was an easy command and something every horse learned early in training. The command for it was to simply pull straight back on the reins—not hard, just steadily. Stevie watched closely.

Garnet was doing exactly what Veronica was telling her to do, which was to turn around.

In the next moment, Garnet and Veronica had taken off on a trail ride. The Saddle Club had never seen anything like it. She just plain rode out of the ring in the middle of the meeting! Even Max, usually completely composed when he was in a riding ring, gaped. Then, becoming aware that he was staring, he returned his attention to the riders in the ring. "Polly," he said. "Tell me three reasons why a horse might need new shoes."

As it turned out, Max, as usual, had planned everything to be fair. All the riders got some questions they could answer, and by listening carefully, they could learn from the other riders as well. One of the youngest members, Lucy Johnson, was the first over the line when she told Max that a rider always mounted from the left-hand side. Everybody clapped for her because she deserved to win and they had all had fun playing the game.

After that, Max took them on a brief trail ride, across a meadow and into the woods behind Pine Hollow. They met up with Veronica in the meadow, where she had been cantering on Garnet. Max called her over to him and everybody heard what he said.

"Veronica, I understand you were excited about riding your new horse for the first time, but leaving the meeting was childish and wrong. Don't do it again."

Then he dismissed her, directing her to the end of the line of riders. As she passed by The Saddle Club, Veronica smiled triumphantly. Stevie shook her head. Veronica actually thought she'd gotten away with something!

CAROLE FINISHED GROOMING Barq and gave him his feed. She was almost ready to find her father and leave for the day. First, though, out of habit, she walked along the hallway between the stalls, looking to see if anyone needed help with his horse. She didn't have to go far before she found somebody who needed a *lot* of help. It was her own father.

Colonel Hanson was standing in Garnet's stall, holding the horse's reins in one hand and examining the bridle as if it were an interesting specimen under a microscope.

"What are you doing?" Carole asked somewhat impatiently. He did look a little stupid standing there.

"I'm trying to figure out how to take this thing off," he cheerfully replied. "Veronica told me she was tired after her ride and asked if I'd take care of her horse for her. I don't mind, but how do you get this thing off?"

"I'll do it," Carole said, speaking more sharply than she meant to. Her father handed her the reins and stood back, watching her.

Carole was upset. Everything seemed wrong to her. How could it be that her very own father, who always knew everything, didn't even know how to remove a bridle? How could he be a good sponsor for Horse Wise—Horse Dumb seemed more apt to her. Even worse, how could it be that somebody who didn't deserve a horse could have one as beautiful and gentle as Garnet?

"Can I help you out there?" Colonel Hanson asked.

"No," Carole said.

"Then maybe I should see if I can help somebody else."

"Sure," she said, although it occurred to her that if she didn't want everybody to know how ignorant he was, it probably wasn't a great idea to send him out as a helper. What was foremost in her mind, though, was Veronica's carelessness. Her carelessness had cost the life of her last horse. What would it do this time?

"NEED SOME HELP?"

Stevie looked up and saw Colonel Hanson standing at the stall door. "Sure, come on in. Help me get Topside untacked."

"Oh, good," he said. "You can show me how to undo this bridle gadget. It's sure got a lot of buckles, doesn't it?"

Stevie laughed. "It's easy. I'll show you. First, you put on a halter—"

"Why do you do that?" he asked.

"Well, you just do," Stevie said, without thinking. She put on the halter first because she always put on a halter first.

"There must be a reason," Colonel Hanson said mildly.

"I suppose," Stevie agreed, and stopped to think about it. "I got it," she said. "You put on a halter and a lead rope so you always have something to control the horse with. A horse like Topside probably doesn't need it, particularly when you're untacking him in his stall, but the time you forget to do it will be the time he's in an open area and he can be out of reach in a second. That's why you should always do it."

"Good," the colonel said, and smiled at Stevie.

Next, she showed him how to remove the saddle. He tried to do it from the horse's right side. Stevie showed him that it should be done from the left.

"Why?" he asked.

Good question, she thought to herself. Saddles were removed from the left because they were always removed from the left. "Actually, I think it's because the horse is used to being approached from the left. It's also the side where most girth adjustments are made, so the leathers are suppler on that side and easier to buckle and unbuckle."

"Makes sense," Colonel Hanson told her.

"Makes sense to me, too," Stevie said. "I never thought about it before, though. I just always did it."

She showed the colonel where to stow the saddle in the tack room and explained the system in there. Then they returned to Topside's stall and began the grooming. It turned out that he didn't know anything

about that, either. Although Stevie had shown many
new riders how to groom and care for a horse, she'd
never had one who asked "why" as often as Carole's
father did.

When the last bit of grooming was finished, and
Topside had fresh hay and fresh water, Stevie turned
to her "instructor" and asked, "Now may I take
twenty-five giant steps for all the right answers I've
given?"

"Why?" he asked, and they both laughed.

8

CAROLE CARRIED GARNET'S saddle and bridle into the tack room, where they would probably stay until Veronica got somebody else to put them on her horse. Carole frowned, thinking again about how upside down the world seemed to be. What she saw when she walked into the tack room made her feel the world was even more upside down. There was her father, the Pony Club sponsor, being instructed on tack cleaning by her friend Lisa.

"No, you just moisten the sponge, you don't wet it," Lisa was saying. "Okay, now rub in small circles. That works the best."

"Why?" the colonel asked.

Carole felt her cheeks flush in embarrassment. Her father didn't know *anything*! She hastily put the tack away and returned to the stable area because she could leave the room that way without being seen by her father or by Lisa. She almost wished that she'd never be seen by anybody ever again. How could she look her friends in the eye after they learned what a dolt her father was when it came to horses?

There were still several Pony Clubbers in the stalls, grooming their horses. Carole needed a place to hide and think a bit. The stalls wouldn't do. She was too likely to be interrupted, or to overhear her father asking more dumb questions. She noticed that the door to the grain room was closed. That meant nobody was in it. It would give her the privacy she needed.

The grain room was actually quite large, but felt small because of the large sacks and bins of grains it held. Carole was always interested in the variety of grains horses were fed. Sometimes, she'd come in here to work with Max on the recipes, which often varied for each horse depending on his individual needs. Today, she ignored the sacks, except to sit on one in a far corner.

The door flew open. One of the younger riders—Carole couldn't remember her name—entered, followed by Carole's father.

"See," the little girl said. "This is the grain room. We give the horses grain as well as hay."

"Well, now. Tell me, why is that?" Carole's father asked.

"I think the grain has more good stuff in it for the horses—like oats, you know. The hay is good, but it's not enough by itself."

"That's a good answer. Thanks, Melanie," the colonel said. Then, for the first time, the two intruders noticed Carole.

"Hi, there, daughter dear," said the colonel. He grinned at Carole.

"Are you *her* dad?" the young rider asked in surprise. Carole cringed.

"Yup!" he answered. Then the two of them left. Her father waved before the door closed. She didn't wave back. Carole put her elbows on her knees and her chin in her hands. As she did so, her hand brushed against her new Pony Club pin. She played with it absently as she thought. The Pony Club was something she wanted to be part of. It was something she cared about. She also cared about her father. He was a terrific dad, but a lousy horseman. These were two very important parts of her life, but they were separate parts, meant to stay that way.

She had to do something. Her father couldn't go on like this. He wasn't any use to the club, and it was embarrassing. Maybe, if her father could take lessons someplace else—not Pine Hollow—and read about a hundred books, then, *maybe* he'd be almost ready to think about being a Horse Wise sponsor. But not now. Not until he was ready to stop asking questions and begin answering them.

Carole realized she might not be the best person to tell her father this. He might not take her seriously, or she might even hurt his feelings. But he would take

Max seriously, and since Max was a professional, her
father wouldn't take his criticism personally. That was
where she would go. Max would understand and help
her. Satisfied that she had the right answer to her
problem, Carole stood up from the sack that had
served as her seat and left the grain room.

"Hi, Carole," Meg Durham greeted her in the stall
hallway. "I was just talking to your dad. I showed him
how to pick a horse's hooves."

"Was he a good student?" Carole asked drily.

Meg giggled.

Carole was sorry she'd asked. She didn't like the
idea of somebody giggling at her dad. She felt as if Meg
were giggling at her!

Max was in the hallway, supervising something in
one of the stalls. Carole needed to talk to him alone.
She walked over to him and waited to get his attention. As soon as she saw what was going on, her heart
sank. Betsy Cavanaugh was showing her father how to
put a leg wrap on a horse.

"Max, can I talk to you—uh, privately?" Carole
asked.

"Sure," he said. A questioning look crossed his face.
"Let's go to my office."

When the door closed on his office, they both sat
down and Carole began. "It's about—"

"I know. Veronica. What she did at the meeting was
totally wrong and then I saw that she really just aban-
doned Garnet and you ended up doing all the work. I

don't think I'm going to be able to change her, you know—"

"It isn't about Veronica," Carole interrupted. "It's about my father."

Max smiled. "It's just great having him here," he said warmly. "He's so enthusiastic! He's got everybody running in circles today. I love it!"

"You love it?" Carole thought she'd heard wrong.

"Every time I turn around, your father is right there, working with another Pony Clubber, one-on-one. It's the best kind of instruction there is. Too few students get it."

"It depends on who is doing the instructing and who is doing the learning," Carole said.

"Oh, absolutely, but I can tell your father really knows how to teach and the riders love him."

"Of course they love him. He's lovable. He's the greatest dad a girl could have. But, well, Max, don't you think it might help him if he had a few, uh, riding lessons or something—you know, somewhere else?"

"No problem there, Carole. I'm doing a weekly class for all of the sponsors. Do you know, some of them really don't know the first thing about horses?"

Now nothing at all made sense to Carole. There was no point in staying in Max's office any longer. Talking to Max wasn't going to help. No matter what anybody else said to her, she knew that her father didn't know what he was doing. He didn't belong at Pine Hollow, and ultimately, he was going to make her look foolish.

The fact that he was a neat, charming guy wouldn't carry him for very long. Eventually, something would have to be done. Carole just hoped she wouldn't have to be the one to do it.

ON MONDAY AFTERNOON, Lisa's parents picked her up once again after school. It was beginning to feel like a comfortable, familiar, but unproductive routine.

This time, the seller was a trainer. Her father had found an ad in the Sunday paper that sounded promising. The horse was a four-year-old bay. Mrs. Atwood was surprised that Lisa was willing to consider a bay, since she thought Lisa only wanted a chestnut. Lisa and her father decided not to try to explain it to her. Mrs. Atwood wasn't stupid, but horse trading was not something that made much sense to her.

"He's a beautiful horse," the trainer, Mr. Michaels, said. One look at the horse and Lisa had to agree. His rich brown coat glistened in the sunshine. "I've been working with him and he learns fast. You're an experienced rider, aren't you, Mr. Atwood?" he asked.

"Me? Not at all. The rider in the family is Lisa. The horse is for her."

"Oh," Mr. Michaels said. Then he furrowed his brow. "I want to sell this horse, but I want the buyer to be happy. This is a good horse and he could be a great show horse someday, but he's young. He needs an excellent rider—one who can continue training him and who has the time and the patience to do it right. I mean, I believe there's championship material here, but I've only been able to start the work. Another year or two, who knows? That's one of the reasons I'm not asking for what I think he'll be worth someday. He really needs more training."

Lisa looked at the horse again. His name was Pretty Boy and she thought it was the perfect name for him.

"Think you want to try him anyway?" Mr. Michaels asked. "I wouldn't blame you."

Lisa nodded. She couldn't resist.

It took a few minutes to tack up Pretty Boy. He fidgeted when the saddle went on and he fought the bit as Mr. Michaels bridled him. Lisa didn't want to notice these things. All she wanted to do was to be in the saddle of the beautiful horse. And very soon, she was. She took the reins in her left hand and climbed on board from the mounting block.

Pretty Boy was tall, dark, and handsome. From where Lisa sat, she was mostly aware of how tall he was. At Pine Hollow, she was used to riding Pepper, who was at least a full hand shorter than Pretty Boy. Horses are measured in hands, which are four-inch units. Pretty Boy pranced about nervously. Lisa leaned forward and patted him on the neck reassuringly. "Easy, boy," she said. He calmed a bit.

"You know what you're doing, I see," Mr. Michaels said. "Now try walking him in a circle. He and I have been working on that."

Lisa signaled the horse with her legs and he responded. She signaled for a right turn and he ignored her. Instead, he stepped backward.

"Be firm," Mr. Michaels said.

Lisa knew that, but it wasn't always easy to do. She signaled again, and he ignored her again. She tapped Pretty Boy on the left front shoulder with her riding crop. At last he turned right and began walking around the ring.

After the second time around the circle, she decided to try a trot. She nudged his belly to get him going. It worked, and he got going, but at a canter, not a trot. For what it was worth, it was a perfectly wonderful canter. Lisa felt as if she were on a rocking chair, gracefully shifting back and forth. But it wasn't what she'd told the horse she wanted him to do. Lisa gave him a slow-down sign with her reins and seat. He slowed to a walk.

It took four more tries to get Pretty Boy to trot and sustain the gait. A trot was a jogging gait and on most horses it was bumpy. Somehow, Pretty Boy managed to do it smoothly.

"Hey, this is a great gait!" Lisa said. "And I love the canter, too, only I don't like it when he wants to canter and I want to trot." Lisa brought Pretty Boy to a walk and rode him over to where her parents and Mr. Michaels were standing.

"That's the problem, isn't it?" Mr. Michaels said.

"Yes, it is. He's a wonderful horse, but not for me."

"You two seem to be speaking a language I don't

understand," Mrs. Atwood said. "What's going on here?"

Lisa tried to explain. "Mom, he's a great horse—or more accurately, he *will* be a great horse, but he's not fully trained. See, what I need is a horse I can ride. I just have a couple of hours a week to ride, and I'd spend them all training, not riding, if we bought Pretty Boy. Now, if you wanted to think about making a pasture out of our backyard and building a stable there, where I could have the horse right there—and maybe have a trainer come two or three hours a day to work with Pretty Boy so he'd be ready for me to ride when I wanted him—"

Mrs. Atwood looked horrified. "Are you actually suggesting that we change our entire—"

"Hold on, there, ma'am," Mr. Michaels said. "Your daughter's right about what it would take, but I think she's joking. She knows this isn't the right horse for her. Am I right?" he asked Lisa.

"Right," she said. "But if he's still for sale when he's five . . ."

"I'm hoping to find Pretty Boy a home for life right now. But I'll keep you in mind."

Lisa dismounted and helped Mr. Michaels untack the horse. As she did, she thought about the kind of owner Pretty Boy should have. She should be an experienced rider, but one not so set in her ways that she wouldn't have fun with a spirited horse. Pretty Boy should belong to somebody who spent a lot of time with horses, maybe even worked with them for a living. He would need a shot at show riding, jumping, and hunting, all kinds of experiences. Lisa hoped very much that Mr. Michaels would be able to find exactly the right person for Pretty Boy.

9

"LISA, YOU'D BETTER come over," Stevie said excitedly on the telephone Tuesday evening. "You've got to see what's happening to my radishes!"

"Radishes? What radishes?" Lisa asked. She had been interrupted in the middle of her history homework and she hadn't yet cleared her brain of the Wars of the Roses to shift into radish gear.

"You know, my *radishes*!" Stevie said insistently.

Then Lisa remembered Stevie's science project. "Oh, *those* radishes. What is it? Is there a problem?"

"No, but they're doing things. You have to see!" Stevie didn't wait for an answer. She hung up the phone.

Lisa giggled to herself. When Stevie got excited about something, no matter what it was, it was almost impossible not to get excited with her. So much for the

Wars of the Roses. She couldn't keep the reds and whites straight from one another anyway.

Lisa grabbed a sweat shirt, told her parents where she was going, and was out the door before anybody could object. She wasn't going far anyway. Stevie's house was just at the other end of the block.

Thinking about Stevie made her think about The Saddle Club and the secret she was keeping from her two best friends. Some secrets were nice, but it depended on whom you were keeping them secret from. Lisa also knew that if she didn't tell her friends, they'd find out about it somehow. Lisa's mother would tell Mrs. diAngelo, who would tell somebody else—maybe even Veronica—and Carole and Stevie would be sure to hear about it. And the only thing worse than keeping a secret from her friends would be having her friends learn about it from somebody else—especially Veronica diAngelo! Lisa had to tell them soon.

"I will," she said out loud to the cool evening. "I'll tell Stevie tonight. Right now, in fact. Then it won't be a horrible secret anymore and I can stop worrying about it." Just saying it out loud made her feel better. She was practically skipping by the time she mounted the steps to Stevie's house, and she was definitely skipping when she climbed the stairs to Stevie's room.

"Look at these guys!" Stevie said, proudly showing Lisa one of her radish pots. "I mean look and see what Mother Nature has done here!"

Lisa dropped her sweat shirt on Stevie's bed and

joined Stevie at her desk, where the lamp on it was totally focused on "Pot Number One: Light and Water." At first, Lisa didn't see a thing. Then, when she took a closer look, she detected quite a few little greenish-white sprouts pushing up through the dirt.

"They're growing!" Stevie said. "It's really working. Aren't they just so cute you can't believe it?"

At first, Lisa thought that cute was a strange word to describe the tiny radish shoots, but the more she thought about it and the more she looked, the more she decided Stevie was right. "Definitely cute," she agreed. "And how about the other pots?"

"Nothing."

"Great, that's just the way it's supposed to be," Lisa said. "See, I told you it would be easy."

"I've decided something," Stevie said. "As soon as this crop of radishes is ready to be harvested, I'll call you and you can come over and have your choice of the bounty of my science experiment. I'll even provide the salt—that is, if you like your radishes with salt. All because you're a real friend."

Lisa knew that Stevie said it to be funny and to thank her. Stevie was being so nice that Lisa felt guilty. It was time to be a real friend and tell Stevie her secret.

Stevie didn't seem to notice that Lisa had something on her mind. "I was at the stable today," she said. "I left my backpack in my cubby after Horse Wise on Saturday. So, of course, I had to go get it because I had my homework assignments written on the back of The Letter, which was still in the backpack. Anyway, guess who else was there? It was good old Veronica diAngelo. Was she there to exercise Garnet and take care of her, groom her, and things like that? No, she was not. She was there because she wanted to check the color of Garnet's blanket against samples she had for a new pair of riding pants and jacket. She wanted to match her clothes to the blanket so they'd be color-coordinated when they had their picture taken together. Can you believe her?"

"No, I can't," Lisa said truthfully. "Sometimes it seems like we've seen everything, but when it comes to Veronica, I'm afraid we haven't even begun to scratch the surface. Some people deserve horses. Veronica definitely doesn't."

Stevie took out the chart she'd devised for noting the progress of her seedlings and carefully measured the tallest of the radish plants. It was three eighths of an inch high. She wrote that down and then wrote large zeros in the other columns. "It feels like a real accomplishment," she announced, replacing the pots on the windowsill. "I'm actually going to have all the information I'm going to need to do this science project right. You are such a pal."

"Thanks," Lisa said. She didn't feel like a pal. Stevie's comment about Veronica and Garnet brought back all of her doubts about sharing her secret. Half an hour later, when Lisa returned to her own room and the Wars of the Roses, she still hadn't told Stevie about her parents' decision to buy her a horse.

"AN IMPORTANT PART of being a Pony Clubber is keeping your own horse's health and maintenance book," Max told the members of Horse Wise the following Saturday.

He handed each club member a folder with individual record sheets in it.

"You'll need to fill these out and bring them to every rating and, even more important, you'll need to keep them up to date. As you'll see, the sheets require certain specific information. Judy is here today to help you all learn how to check on your horse's health and fill out these sheets . . ."

As Max continued talking, Carole looked at her booklet. It was designed to be a year-long log of everything from the horse's basic health, like his normal pulse rate and temperature, to the veterinary visits, cost of horse care, and income of the rider. Carole knew about the care book from the last time she'd been in a Pony Club.

"The first thing we need to do is to learn how to check a horse's pulse," Judy said. "Colonel Hanson, can you show us how to do this?"

Carole felt a nervous twinge in her stomach. If her father had read one of the three books she'd left on his bedside table last week, he might, just might, have learned what to do. Otherwise, it was going to be another embarrassing moment for her. She held her breath.

The colonel stepped forward to where Judy held Patch, a black-and-white pinto, by his lead rope. To Carole's dismay, he grinned and reached down and put his hand against Patch's foreleg, as if it were the horse's wrist.

Carole groaned out loud. Nobody heard it, though. Everybody was laughing too loud. Carole hung back in a corner, hoping that nobody could see her, hoping, in fact, that nobody would know she existed.

"Nice try, Colonel," Judy said. "But you flunk." More giggles. "Anybody want to show this man what to do?"

A few hands went up. Judy called on Stevie. Stevie showed Colonel Hanson and everybody else the two easiest places to check a horse's pulse. The first was in between the animal's jawbones, at the curve of the cheek. The second was on the horse's belly, right behind his elbow.

Stevie put her hand under Patch's jaw, checked Judy's watch, which had a sweep-second hand, and counted the beats for fifteen seconds.

"Twelve," she announced. "Multiply it by four and get, uh—" She looked at Lisa, frantically. Lisa just gave her a dirty look. "Oh, yeah, forty-eight," Stevie concluded sheepishly.

Judy and everybody else laughed. Then Judy had everybody come and check Patch's pulse rate. When all the Pony Clubbers had done it, she turned back to Colonel Hanson. "Think you can do it now?" she asked.

"I'll try," he said, and then, to Carole's relief, did it correctly.

Judy then proceeded to demonstrate how to check the horse's respiration or breathing rate. This is important for a rider to know, because the respiration rate, among other things, is an indication of whether a horse is overheated or not. After Judy had completed her instruction, each rider was told to fill in the record book for his own horse.

Carole picked up a pencil and headed for Barq's stall. Barq wasn't her very own horse, of course, but he was the horse she had been riding most recently at Pine Hollow. The horse she had ridden before Barq was Delilah, a palomino mare who was a wonderful horse to ride. But she had just foaled a few months earlier and was spending her days with her colt, Samson. Samson's sire, or father, had been Veronica's stallion, Cobalt. Carole had to pass their little stall and paddock on her way to Barq's. She noticed Samson frolicking around the paddock, obviously in a good and playful mood. Delilah stood serenely nearby, watching him with one eye, and nibbling at grass sprouts. Sometimes horses seemed very human to Carole, and this was one of those times. Samson was like a rambunctious toddler, and Delilah his overtired mother. The sight made Carole smile for the first time since the Horse Wise meeting had been called to order.

She continued to Barq's stall. It took her only a few minutes to check his condition and jot down the figures. Then she had to draw his significant markings. For Carole, that would take a little longer. Barq was a bay with Arabian blood, and he had a white blaze on his face that looked like a streak of lightning. That was how he got his name, because *Barq* meant lightning in Arabic. It was a tricky marking to draw. Carole turned over his water bucket, sat on it, and studied the horse so she could draw it properly. Drawing was not one of Carole's strongest talents. In fact, she doubted that she'd be able to draw it properly no matter how hard she tried.

"Rats," she said, breaking the point of her pencil on the point of the lightning streak. She'd have to go to Mrs. Reg's office to sharpen it. Carefully, she fastened the stall door behind her and walked toward the office.

The whole stable was bustling with activity as all the Horse Wise members were trying to complete the work in their health-and-maintenance books. Judy was helping one young rider take her horse's temperature. Stevie was checking to see if Topside had a tattoo. Even Veronica was working. She was sketching in Garnet's color. Since she was a solid chestnut, it was fairly easy to do, but Carole had to give Veronica some credit. It was work.

While Carole was sharpening her pencil, her father

came into the tack room, which adjoined Mrs. Reg's office.

"Oh, there you are," he said. "Listen, Max wants to have a short sponsors' meeting after Horse Wise is dismissed. Would you mind waiting around for me?"

"No problem," she said. She really didn't mind, and besides, it would give her a chance to talk with Stevie and Lisa alone.

"Thanks," he said. "And one other thing—what's normal temperature for a horse?"

"Ninety-nine and a half to a hundred and a half," Carole answered automatically.

"Oh, good," he said. "I thought that little fellow out there might be coming down with something and I wasn't sure what I should do for him. But it's just a normal temperature."

"What were you going to do if he had been sick?" Carole asked out of curiosity. She was sorry the minute she asked.

"Oh, you know, the usual. Tea and cinnamon toast and he can stay home from school one day, but he'd have to see the doctor to be allowed to stay home any longer than that."

Carole knew, beyond any doubt, that he'd used that line on whatever Pony Clubber he was "helping." It was his rule of thumb whenever Carole got sick at home. It made sense at home and always made her laugh, too. But that was at home. This was at Pine

Hollow. They weren't the same at all. Carole knew that. Why didn't her father?

She didn't know what to say to him, so she decided not to say anything. "See you later," she said, escaping to the privacy of Barq's stall. On her way there, she found Stevie and Lisa and told them they *had* to have a Saddle Club meeting in the tack room after Horse Wise. While her father was busy, she could use the time to apologize to her friends for his dumb behavior. She hoped they would understand.

STEVIE TOOK TOPSIDE'S saddle off its storage rack and rested it on the bench in front of her so she could clean it. She'd finished her Horse Wise work before her friends and was able to get a head start on cleaning tack. She was already working on the stirrup leathers by the time Carole and Lisa arrived.

"You know, I think I preferred it this summer when we could ride every day, not just twice a week," Stevie told them.

"Of course you did!" Lisa said, laughing. "Riding five or six times a week is *much* better than going to school."

"For once, that isn't what I mean," Stevie said. "It's that there's so much to learn about horses. I don't think you can learn all you need to know twice a week—even with Horse Wise, which, by the way, I love a lot!"

"Me, too," Lisa agreed. "Everybody does. Even Veronica was doing something for Garnet when I passed her stall."

"Not something really tricky like untacking her, was it?" Stevie asked sarcastically.

"No, she was patting her," Lisa admitted.

"Well, that's a step," Carole said. "I didn't think she knew that much about horse care." Carole shook her head in disbelief. "Why her parents ever bought her another horse—especially a horse like Garnet—is beyond me."

"Well, because they could afford it," Lisa offered tentatively.

"Money isn't the issue," Carole snapped. Lisa and Stevie looked at her in surprise. "Well, I suppose in Veronica's case, it *always* is. But that's not what I mean. You shouldn't get a horse because you can afford it, or because your parents think you're wonderful, or because you can talk them into it. You should get a horse because you can take care of it, because you know the things you need to know, because you can be responsible for it."

Carole picked up Barq's bridle and began polishing it vigorously. She continued talking. "The thing is that I don't envy a lot of stuff Veronica has, like the big house and the designer clothes and all that. But I *do* envy her owning Garnet. It makes me so angry because I don't understand it. She's a pretty good rider, all right, but she doesn't know the first thing about taking care of her."

"You have to deserve a horse," Stevie agreed.

"Anyway, that reminds me of what I wanted to talk to you guys about," Carole said. "My father."

"You deserve him!" Stevie said. "He's just wonderful. We all adore him, you know."

Carole looked at her quizzically. "I guess I do know, but what I don't know is, why? I mean, Horse Wise is about getting wise about horses, not answering his 'whys' all the time. He knows less than Veronica does. It's really embarrassing."

Stevie was surprised by Carole's words. It had never occurred to her that Carole could be embarrassed by Colonel Hanson. Stevie could be embarrassed by her parents all the time. But her parents were *parents*. They did typical things like believing her brothers, or telling Stevie she couldn't ride if she didn't study first, or even telling her teacher that she *hadn't* read the book that she'd written the A report on. *That* was embarrassing. But Colonel Hanson told corny old jokes and sang Elvis Presley by heart. He was just wonderful!

"Of course he doesn't know anything," Stevie said. "He's never had a chance to learn, but he sure is learning now. You know, I only had to show him once how to assemble a bridle and he had it. He even remembered the names of all the parts. You should have seen him showing that little boy in Horse Wise, Liam, how to mount his pony. Your dad was terrific. And he did it right, too. And he made it fun. Your dad—"

Stevie thought she could have gone on for hours about how great Colonel Hanson was. She also had the feeling that if she did, Carole would never speak to her again. Whatever it was that Stevie thought about Carole's dad, Carole didn't seem to agree. Stevie paused to think about it, exploring the possibilities as she finished soaping the saddle's skirt. Their silence was interrupted by Max's arrival. Max didn't look very happy. In fact, he looked a little frantic.

"Oh, good, girls, I thought I would find you here. I need some help. Someone took off on a trail ride across the fields and left the paddock gates open behind them. Samson's on the loose. Can you saddle up and help find him?"

Max didn't have to ask twice. Each girl took her partially cleaned tack and ran back to her horse's stall. Stevie had Topside tacked up in about three minutes. She was still tightening the girth when she met her friends at the door to the stable. A little colt could get into a lot of trouble in a very short time. There wasn't a minute to waste!

"Let's go!" Stevie said.

"Wait a minute, we need to take a few things with us," Carole said rationally.

"A halter for Samson," Lisa suggested. "And a lead rope."

"Not a bad idea," Carole agreed. "Though he's barely used to the halter and it might not work. But you're right. We ought to have them with us."

"The first-aid kit, just in case?" Stevie offered.

"Yeah, good idea," Lisa said. "I'll go get it from the tack room. And some extra ropes, too. You never know."

"And one other thing," Carole said.

"What's that?" Lisa asked.

"Delilah," Carole said.

Of course, Stevie thought. There was one thing that would be more appealing than anything else in the world to a lost or frightened colt, and that was his mother.

Quickly, Carole snapped a long lead rope on Delilah and fastened it to Barq's saddle. Delilah was a well-trained horse. She would follow along willingly.

"One more thing," Lisa said to her friends. Stevie wondered what it was they might have forgotten. "The good-luck horseshoe," Lisa said.

"Once for us and once for Samson," Stevie said, brushing the horseshoe twice as she passed by. The shiny, smooth surface seemed reassuring to her.

Then they were off!

As its name implied, Pine Hollow was surrounded by hills. They weren't very steep, but there were a lot of them. While the hills made it easy to look up and inspect the nearby fields, they made it very difficult to see anything farther than a couple of hundred yards in every direction. Also, since Max had made arrangements with many nearby farmers to ride in their fields, as long as fences were opened and closed properly, it was just about impossible to figure out which direction the rider might have taken. There were signs of horse paths everywhere they looked.

"We just have to follow the open fences," Carole said logically. "And we have to hope that the rider didn't leave them *all* open. As soon as we find the closed one, we've got Samson located, more or less. Then, with some luck, Delilah will do the rest of the work for us, right?"

"Sounds good, except for one thing," Stevie said. Carole recognized Stevie's bad-news tone of voice. "There's only one rider at Pine Hollow who would waft out into the fields without thinking about closing fences behind her."

Carole and Lisa supplied the answer at the same time. "Veronica diAngelo," they said.

"Yeah, and she would not only leave one fence open behind her. She'd leave *every* fence open behind her. Let's face it. If she stays in the fields, Samson will probably be okay, because at least he'll be contained in an open area. The worst thing, though, would be if she went into the woods up on the hill, because once she goes through the last fence up there, there are no more fences."

"Oh, no! The highway!" Lisa said. "Those woods run right by the interstate, don't they?"

95

"Yes, they do," Carole said. "And they're very thick woods up there where a little inexperienced colt could get into a lot of trouble! There's no time to waste! Let's go!"

The decision, then, was an easy one. Since the worst possible outcome was that Samson could have made his way into the woods, they had to go there first. If he didn't turn out to be there, but *did* turn out to be in one of the fields, that could be tricky, but at worst, wouldn't really be dangerous to Samson.

Carole had learned that horses seemed to be able to sense urgency, whether it was to win a competition of some kind or to act in an emergency. Most horse books she'd read said they weren't especially smart animals, but they sure did seem to understand certain things at certain times. This was one of those times. If Carole hadn't been able to hear all four of Barq's hooves hitting the ground as they rode up the rise, she would have sworn they were flying. Delilah kept right up with them, and Stevie and Lisa were right behind her.

Ironically, their trip was sped up by the fact that, as they went from field to field, they only had to pause to close the gates behind them. The way was easy for them—and for Samson—courtesy of Miss Veronica diAngelo.

And then they spotted Veronica. She was having a wonderful time. She and Garnet were cantering in a field next to the woods. It was one of the most level fields in the area, a logical choice for somebody who just wanted to canter. Carole pursed her lips in anger. It was so babyish to think that the most fun you could have on a horse was cantering, just because it was fast. In the first place, it wasn't true. Having fun on a horse meant learning to work *with* the horse, not getting the horse to do all the work. A horse wasn't a race car. In the second place, constantly cantering wore a horse out. Garnet would do what Veronica told her to do, but she'd be tired for days, and could stiffen up badly. Carole wanted to give Veronica a good lecture on her behavior. She would have, but Samson was more important. And Samson was nowhere in sight.

Carole looked at Delilah hopefully. The mare would know where her colt was before anybody could see him. Delilah just looked forlorn and confused. She whinnied. Carole knew she was calling for Samson. There was no answer.

"Where could he be?" Carole asked Stevie and Lisa, who drew their horses to a halt where she was standing. "If Veronica's here, then he can't have gone any farther, can he?"

"Not unless Veronica did," Lisa said logically.

Then, all three of them looked at the fence along the edge of the woods. The gate stood wide open.

"I'd like to give that girl a piece of my mind!" Stevie burst out angrily.

"Me, too, but first things first. Let's find Samson!" Carole said.

She gave Barq a signal and once again, he flew into action.

It irked Carole more than she could say to see Veronica wave to them gaily as they went through the open gate into the woods. Veronica had no idea how much trouble she had caused. She probably wouldn't care when she found out, either.

A four-month-old colt is a curious animal. Carole found herself making lists of ways he could get into trouble—everything from eating poisonous plants, to tripping and breaking a fragile young limb. Sometimes people reported seeing bobcats in these woods. Even worse, sometimes there were hunters, looking for deer, in *and* out of season. A colt was about the size of the local deer. There was a dreadful cold feeling in her stomach.

"Whatever you're thinking, stop it," Stevie said sensibly. "We'll find him. He'll be okay."

It didn't surprise Carole that Stevie could read her mind. Stevie was probably feeling the same way, and so was Lisa. Carole took comfort in the fact that the three of them together seemed to have a way of solving some pretty terrible problems. It wasn't just strength in numbers, because three wasn't a very large number. It was the power of their friendship. That was what The Saddle Club was about. But would friendship be enough this time?

Suddenly, Delilah's ears perked up. Her nostrils flared. She halted, bringing Barq to a sudden stop. Carole watched the mare carefully. She was their leader now.

Delilah pawed the ground and whinnied. Her ears flicked around, listening for a return signal. She took two steps up the hill, and the girls followed. Delilah glanced at Carole. On a hunch, Carole unclipped the mare's lead rope. Carole had the feeling that Delilah was so well trained that she wouldn't run away from her human masters as long as she felt close to them. Without the rope, she could follow her instincts and they would surely lead her to her colt.

For a moment Delilah stood frozen. The girls were silent, waiting. Then Delilah whinnied again, calling to her son. She raised her head high, trying to make the sound carry. Then she waited.

A rustling sound came from the leaves down the hill a bit to the left. The girls eagerly turned their heads in that direction. A squirrel emerged from a pile of leaves and skittered up a tree.

Tentatively, Delilah began to walk up the hill, ducking under branches, and squeezing between trees. There was no way anyone riding could follow her. The girls dismounted and led their horses after Delilah, making as little noise as possible so the mare could hear what she was listening for.

Delilah's pace picked up. Her ears flicked to the left and she turned that way, going straight now. She whinnied louder and repeatedly. Her tail twitched excitedly, and her head bobbed, as she tried to see everything in range.

Then she stopped and whinnied loudly. And, for

the first time, the girls could hear Samson's reply. It was little more than a whimper. The girls wrapped their horses' reins around firm branches, and ran over to see where Samson was.

He'd fallen into a gully totally overgrown with briars. His legs were completely tangled in the mass of leaves and sharp green shoots. He was lying down and seemed to be crying. His slender legs had been poked and torn at repeatedly by the vicious weeds. Blood trickled out of his wounds.

They'd found Samson, all right, but were they too late to save him?

"WHERE DO WE begin?" Stevie asked, aghast.

"We begin by freeing him," Carole said sensibly. Carole, who could sometimes be flaky when it came to anything else, was all common sense with horses. She could keep a cool head in emergencies.

"Okay," she began, knowing her friends needed some assurance. "We helped bring this little guy into the world and it's our job to keep him here." It sounded good. Somehow knowing that Samson and her friends were relying on her helped. Her mind was sharp, her mission clear. "Stevie, are you carrying your pocketknife?"

"Of course," Stevie said and handed it to Carole.

"Here's how we're going to do this. I'm going to work on cutting the briars. Stevie, you stay by Samson's head and do whatever you can to keep him calm. I don't want him kicking me if we can help it. Lisa, you put the lead rope back on Delilah and tie her up where she can watch, but not interfere. Stay with her for a while until we're sure she'll stay calm. The last thing we need on our hands is a hysterical mother!"

Stevie and Lisa laughed at Carole's joke. It was good for all of the girls. It broke some of the tension. Carole opened Stevie's old Girl Scout knife and surveyed the situation. The briar was the kind that was like a tough philodendron with stickers on the stems. Once you stepped into it, it acted almost like a Chinese finger trap and there was no getting out without some kind of scratch. Carole quickly realized that she wouldn't be able to keep Samson from getting hurt, and began to see her job as trying to keep him from getting hurt badly. She was going to need his cooperation as much as her friends'.

Samson had slid into a gully where the briar was flourishing. The good news was that he hadn't slid very far. He was lying on his side, and all four of his legs and his tail were entangled.

First things first: Carole needed to know if he had any wounds worse than scratches. Slowly and carefully, to minimize her own scratching, she lowered herself into the gully and sat down next to the colt. He looked at her fearfully. His eyes were wide open and white at the edges.

"There, there, boy," Carole said soothingly. "Take it easy, now. I'm just going to check you out and then get you out." His eyes closed a little bit and he seemed to relax.

"He trusts our voices," Stevie said.

"Maybe because they were the first sounds he ever heard when he was born. Do you think that means he thinks we're his mother?" Lisa asked. At that moment, Delilah whinnied and Samson answered with his own small cry.

"No, I think he knows who his mother is. He just thinks we're a team of capable humans who helped him out of one jam and are going to help him make it out of this one," Carole said. She hoped Samson was right. She began her task.

"What's the first step?" Lisa asked.

"I'm feeling his legs to make sure we're not dealing with any broken bones here. I can also see if any of the cuts are deep."

"Why?"

"Well, if he's losing a lot of blood from something, I won't have time to cut away gently. We'll have to slash at the briars and take our chances on giving him fresh wounds in order to get him out as fast as possible."

Carole clipped a few of the briar's tendrils, snagging her hands as she went. She was closest to Samson's left foreleg. As soon as she could, she reached down and ran her hand along the outside of it. It felt moist, but okay. She felt along the inside, coming back up. "No problem there," she reported to her friends. "Yet."

They were in a very shady area of the woods, and the autumn sun was beginning to sink in the sky, casting long shadows through the forest. Along with all of the other problems they had, Carole couldn't see very well. She was going to have to do the entire check on Samson with her hands.

She reached into the briar again, groping for his right foreleg. "Ouch!" she said. Samson flinched at the sound of her voice.

"Problem?" Stevie asked with concern.

"It's me, not him," Carole told her. "I just got scratched. It's not serious. It just hurts."

"Pull your sleeves down," Stevie suggested.

"Now, why didn't I think of that?" Carole said, withdrawing her scratched arm from the tangle of briars. She tugged her shirtsleeves down and hoped they'd stay that way. "I wish I were wearing one of Dad's shirts today. They're so big, they always come down over your hands."

"Wait a minute," Stevie said. "I think I can help with that. I've got my riding gloves—the ones you guys gave me."

"But they'll get ruined. Those are really nice gloves," Carole protested.

"And you are a really good friend," Stevie reminded her. "Your hands are a lot more important than my gloves."

"Okay. I'm not going to argue. I need all the help I can get." Gratefully, Carole pulled the gloves on, noticing that there was blood on her hands. Was it her own blood or Samson's? Probably some of both, she told herself. She reached back in to check the second foreleg. This time, she felt the sticking of the briar, but it only scratched at the leather glove.

"The gloves help a lot," Carole said. "Thanks, Stevie."

"You're very welcome," Stevie said. "And besides, you gave those to me for my birthday. Christmas is just around the corner. You won't have to think for very long to come up with something for that!"

Carole smiled and was about to come up with a retort for Stevie's remark when she found that Samson's right foreleg was lying in a very awkward position. She didn't like that at all. The leg was bent too high, as if he were reaching for something. Did that mean he had a broken bone? The elbow and forearm were fine, although they were stretched out of position. It didn't make sense. Then, as Carole got to the fetlock, she realized that the colt's leg was hooked on a root that protruded from the ground. It was quite possible that that alone was keeping Samson from sliding farther down the steep sides of the gully.

Samson's leg was scratched, but intact, as far as Carole could tell, but the fact that it was hooked onto something was dangerous.

While Carole shifted her position to examine Samson's rear legs, she turned to Lisa. "If Delilah's okay for a while, could you go to my saddle and get the ropes? I'm afraid Samson may shift around and slide much deeper into this place." She spoke calmly so she wouldn't alarm the colt, but the message to her friend was clear. Lisa wasted no time in following Carole's instructions.

While Lisa retrieved the ropes, Carole checked Samson's hind legs. There was at least one fairly deep scratch on one of them, but it didn't seem to be bleeding too badly. Carole proceeded with her original plan. She began cutting at the briars, silently thanking Stevie for the gloves with every painless snip.

Lisa returned with the ropes. "Here they are, but how are we going to manage this?"

Carole thought about it for a minute. She hadn't been sure exactly what she had in mind when she sent Lisa for the ropes. That part just seemed logical. But what was the next logical step? "What I want to do is to get at least one rope, preferably two, around his belly so that we have him in a sort of a sling in case his leg unhooks from this root here. The problem is that he's pretty heavy and maybe just trying to put the ropes under him will dislodge him. But it's a risk we've got to take."

Stevie stayed at her post, keeping Samson quiet. She stroked his neck and sang to him.

"Good job, Stevie. Keeping him calm is more important than ever now," Carole said, though she was sure Stevie knew that without being told.

"And it's a good thing he likes Beatles songs. I thought 'Hey Jude' was a good idea."

Carole laughed. Jude, as she knew, was the saint of impossible causes. She hoped Samson's rescue wasn't an impossible cause! She quickly used Stevie's knife to cut two lengths of rope, each about twelve feet long.

Lisa held one end of each of the lengths of rope. Carole slid the other ends under Samson's hindquarters, bringing one forward to his front legs and leaving the other at his rear. He didn't seem to like it, but he let her do it. Carole sighed with relief as she passed the rope ends to Lisa.

"Very good!" Lisa said. "I don't know how you did that!"

"I'm not sure I do, either," Carole said. "But it worked, didn't it?"

Just then, Samson announced that he'd had enough. He began to flail around wildly, rocking his head, jostling Stevie, and kicking violently.

This was good news and bad news. The bad

news was that, exactly as Carole had predicted, he unhooked his foreleg from the root and began sliding down farther into the gully. The good news was that, because of Carole's foresight, they'd already planned for that. Lisa held both of the rope loops by herself until Carole scrambled up the hill to help her.

The two girls not only held Samson up, keeping him from slipping farther, but they began stepping backward, away from the gully, tugging Samson upward as they went. The colt struggled to get a purchase on the loose dirt, crying out a couple of times as briars scratched at him, but within a few seconds, he was able to scramble his way up the hillside, out of the dangerous briar patch.

"Give him a hand!" Carole cried to Stevie. Stevie jumped to her feet and grabbed Samson's scruffy mane. She pulled as hard as she could, knowing that she wasn't hurting him because a horse doesn't have any nerves in those hair roots. He certainly didn't seem to mind.

When Samson had gotten his front legs up over the top of the gully, Carole handed her rope to Lisa and went to check the progress of his hind legs. One of them, the one with the deep scratch, was still tangled in a briar. Carole reached over the edge and yanked at the weed. She hoped she had made enough slack to allow Samson to free himself. It worked!

By the time Carole turned around, Samson was standing at the top of the gully, free from all briars, panting with fatigue, but safe.

There was nothing Carole wanted to do more right then than hug Samson and her friends with joy and relief, but she knew the work wasn't finished. They couldn't take the chance, however slight, that something might make Samson run back into the gully. While Stevie and Lisa patted him and led him away from the edge of the gully, Carole retrieved Samson's halter and lead.

"Are you going to put those on him?" Lisa asked, a little surprised.

"We have to," Carole said. "We just can't take a chance with him now. Once he's in the field, we can let him loose. Until then, it's halter or bust."

Carole knew from experience with Samson's earliest training that Samson sometimes fought when the halter was put on him. Sometimes, he'd shake his head quite violently. He just wasn't accustomed to it. So Carole was more than a little nervous.

"What can we do to make him not notice the halter, then?" Lisa asked.

Carole thought for a second. "Delilah!" she exclaimed. "Bring his mother here. He's really too tired to put up much of a fight, and I'll bet you anything his stomach is empty and he's starving. Bring on the Nursing Mama!"

Laughing, Stevie unhitched Delilah and reunited

her with her son. The mare checked him thoroughly, sniffing and nuzzling him, apparently trying to be absolutely certain that this dusty, dirty, scratched-up colt was really her little baby. While the two of them got reacquainted, Carole slipped the halter on Samson and clipped on a lead rope. He didn't pay any attention to her. When Delilah was satisfied that the colt was her lost son, she allowed him to nurse.

"Look at his poor legs," Lisa said, watching the procedure. "Are they going to be okay?"

Carole examined them carefully. "Probably," she said. "There's only one deep scratch and it seems to be closing naturally. However, we could have an infection problem, which would be a lot worse than scarring. Let's get the first-aid kit and kill some germs."

While Samson was concentrating on his meal, Stevie sprayed his legs with the disinfectant, Lisa applied scarlet oil, and Carole wrapped his legs in bandages.

"Hey, check this out!" Stevie said softly, trying not to disturb their patient. "We're all nursing. Samson's doing the baby kind of nursing and we're three Clara Bartons out here on the battlefield of horse care!"

Lisa and Carole laughed, both because it was funny, and because they felt good. They'd done something important and they'd done it right.

"Isn't it wonderful that Samson's okay?" Lisa asked. "What a job you did!" she told Carole admiringly.

"In the first place, *we* did it, not just me," Carole corrected her. "In the second place, we're not quite done."

"Oh, sure," Stevie said. "Judy's going to want to rebandage all the cuts, maybe take some stitches . . ."

"No, before that," Carole said. "Look at Samson."

The colt licked the last splash of milk from his lips and then glanced around. The look was unmistakable. He was ready for his nap. He would never make it back to Pine Hollow and there was no way they could carry him safely.

The girls decided to make him walk with Delilah, at least as far as the safety of the first fence in the fields. Then they would wait with him until help arrived. Max was sure to come looking for them with his truck. Until then, no harm would come to any of them.

A few minutes later, The Saddle Club settled into the sweet grass, not far from Samson, and waited, glad for the quiet and the rest.

Samson was asleep before Carole could get the halter off of him.

12

"STAR LIGHT, STAR bright, first star I've seen to-night," Stevie said, looking up into the early-evening sky. It was still light out, but the evening star was clearly visible above the southern horizon.

"I know what I'm wishing for," Lisa said, staring up into the sky as well. The minute she said it, she knew it was time to tell her friends her secret. They waited for her to continue. "I'm wishing for words to tell you something I haven't been able to tell you."

"Bad news?" Stevie asked, alarmed.

"No, just hard to figure out. Hard to talk about. But I think I've figured it out now, so I can talk about it." There was a long silence. Lisa continued to look at the sky as she spoke. "My parents had this idea about buying me a horse. I think my mother got the idea because she heard the diAngelos were buying Garnet for Veronica. We even looked at three different horses."

"And you didn't tell us?" Stevie asked. She sounded hurt.

Lisa knew she deserved that, if not a lot more. "No, I didn't. And I felt terrible keeping it from you." Lisa took a deep breath. "I want a horse. It's my dream. The problem was that something told me it wasn't right. And the problem with that was I didn't know what the 'something' was. So I developed this wild notion that you two would be jealous."

"Well, we would be, of course," Stevie said. "But we'd understand."

"That's the part I forgot. Of course you'd understand. Now I know that, but I also know that it's still a bad idea. See, I was concentrating so hard on the idea that you were jealous of Veronica that I forgot what the real reason was for Veronica not to have a horse."

"And that is?" Carole asked.

Lisa had the feeling Carole knew the answer and was testing her. "Because she doesn't know enough about horses to care for her own properly," Lisa answered.

"Go to the head of the class," Carole said.

"Thanks. It took me a long time, but the lesson Veronica gave about responsibility by bad example was as clear as a bell."

"But Lisa, you're more responsible than Veronica," Stevie said.

"Thanks, but a lamppost is more responsible than Veronica. I think I do all right on that part. The part that I'm not so good on is just plain horse knowledge. I'm learning. I know I'm learning, but that's not enough yet. One day, I will have learned enough. Until then, I'm going to thank my parents for the wonderful idea and I'll happily continue riding Pepper."

Carole smiled. "I think you're absolutely right, except about one thing. It's not going to be as far in the future as you may think. You're learning at an amazing rate."

"Becoming horse wise, you mean," Stevie contributed. "Speaking of which, Horse Wise should be helpful. I was looking through *The Manual of Horsemanship*—you know, the Pony Club book Max gave us. Being Pony Clubbers is certainly going to speed up that day for all of us."

Carole sighed audibly.

"What's the matter?" Lisa asked. She was relieved that she'd gotten her troubles off her chest. She hated to think that something was bothering Carole so much that she had to sigh like that!

"Horse Wise," Carole said and then sighed again. "If the stars are granting wishes tonight, I know what my wish is."

"What?" Stevie asked.

"You may not believe this, but my wish is to have Dad not be a Horse Wise sponsor anymore."

Stevie propped herself up on her elbow. "I don't get it, Carole. You've got one of the neatest fathers this side of the Mississippi. Why don't you want him to be a sponsor?"

"Sure, he's a neat guy. He's good at being a father and a Marine, but he's not good at horses. Sponsors are supposed to be able to teach. He can't teach anybody anything about horses because he doesn't know anything."

"Now, wait a minute. He's teaching everybody! He's *terrific*," Lisa said.

"Lisa, you're supposed to be the logical one in this group. That's just not logical," Carole responded.

"No, look at it from our standpoint, Carole," Lisa persisted. "We know your father doesn't know anything about horses, but he *does* know about teaching—and learning. See, what your dad does is make us think. Every time he asks why, two things happen. First, we have to think about what we're doing, and that gives us information. Second, we have to tell him and that gives *him* information. Don't worry, Carole, he's not just neat, he's smart. Before too long, he'll stop asking because he doesn't know and begin asking just to make sure we *do*. That is, if he's not doing that already. In the meantime, what difference does it make?"

Carole couldn't think of a reply so she just stared up

at the sky, which was now becoming a deep, rich blue.
A few more stars had appeared. There was an autumn
chill in the late-afternoon air.

Carole's mind was a jumble. She tried to sort it all
out. She wasn't quite satisfied that her friends were
right about her father, though she accepted the fact
that everybody liked him. But was that enough? Not
really. In order for him to be a good sponsor, he had to
contribute some skills to Horse Wise. No matter what
her friends told her, Carole didn't see what skills her
father had contributed.

Nearby, Samson snorted in his sleep. He seemed to
be content and worry-free.

"I think he's dreaming about a palomino filly," Lisa
joked.

"Either that or the world-famous Saddle Club Rescue Team," Stevie suggested. "A couple more jobs like
the one we did this afternoon and we'll have our own
TV show. I can see it now. How about *The Saddle Club
Files?*"

"Nah, we need something jazzier. *Saddle Club
SWAT?*"

"I've got it! *The Saddle Club to the Rescue!*" Stevie
suggested.

"It's not punchy enough," Lisa said. "It has to fit on
one line in bold type in *TV Guide*. How about . . ."

The conversation went on like that, but Carole
dropped out of it. She was thinking about Samson's
rescue. She remembered how worried and scared she

had felt, lodged onto the edge of the gully with a foal just as worried and just as scared as she was. Every time she hadn't known what to do, Lisa had asked her what came next. Every time she'd thought she'd known what she might do, Lisa had asked why she was doing it. Lisa's questions had had a good effect. They'd made Carole think about what she was doing. She probably would have figured it out on her own, but having Lisa there to ask had made her consider the problem in a new way and think about the answers.

Maybe, just maybe, that was what her father was doing in Horse Wise. Maybe having one sponsor who didn't know about horses, but who did know about thinking and learning, wasn't such a bad idea after all.

Only why couldn't it be someone else's father?

"Well, I'm going to make a prediction. I predict Max will show up before the temperature drops another ten degrees," Stevie was saying.

Lisa sat up and looked out across the fields. "Well, if those headlights are any indication, your prediction has just come true!"

"Impressed?" Stevie asked.

"Yeah," Lisa said. "Very."

"Don't be," Carole said drily. "Remember that Stevie's taller than you are. She could see those headlights before you could."

"And I thought Stevie was clairvoyant!" Lisa joked.

The girls stood up to wave at Max. He spotted them right away and within a very short time, they had loaded the still-sleeping foal into the back of the pickup truck, where Judy was waiting to take care of him. They tied Delilah's lead rope behind the truck. Max would have to drive slowly, but it made more sense than trying to separate mother and son again.

While the truck lumbered off down the dirt road toward the stable, the girls tightened their horses' girths, lowered their stirrups, and mounted their animals. It was time for them to ride back as well—checking every fence gate on the way.

STEVIE COULD HARDLY believe it was just a week since The Saddle Club's dramatic rescue of Samson. Except for one remaining bandage, which covered three stitches in one of his hind legs, there were no signs that anything bad had ever happened to the colt. He was frolicking around his well-closed paddock with his mother, happy as could be.

Stevie wished she could be as calm. She was a nervous wreck. It was Horse Wise Rating Day.

Since this was the first rating, each person had been allowed to choose what rating he or she wanted to be tested for. Stevie had decided, without looking at the test requirements, that she was certainly a D-3. That was what she'd signed up for. *Then* she looked at the requirements. If she failed the test, she'd be unrated until the next rating. That would be pretty embarrassing. The only rider in the stable who was going to be unrated was seven-year-old Liam, who had just started riding the day of the first Horse Wise meeting.

"Stevie Lake." The examiner called her name.

Stevie felt a severe twinge in her stomach. She shook it off and tried to concentrate. She stepped forward into the ring, riding Topside. The riding test was the easy part. She wasn't worried about that, and within fifteen minutes, she'd performed everything the examiner had asked her to do, including mounting and dismounting, adjusting stirrups, walking and trotting in circles, and changing speeds within gaits. The jumps were no problem at all. She knew she'd passed that section.

Then came the unmounted part of the test. The Pony Club called it Horse Management. Stevie called it The Tough Part. Carole and Lisa had been drilling her all week on horse parts, conformation faults, and coat-clipping techniques. Phil had done the same when they talked on the phone. Stevie knew she could name all the major bones of the horse's legs. She just wasn't sure she knew which was which.

She hoped the examiner wouldn't ask her.

"Good, Stevie," he said, after she told him how to cool down her horse after a ride. "Now, show me the major bones of the legs—fore and hind."

They were the very words she'd been dreading. "Okay," Stevie said, thinking it wasn't okay at all.

Then she looked around and saw that both Lisa and Carole were standing at the edge of the ring watching, with their fingers crossed. What more could a girl want than to have friends like that? She *couldn't* let them down.

"Top to bottom or bottom to top?" she asked.

"Whichever," the examiner said.

Stevie squatted and began with Topside's hoof. "Coffin, navicular, short pastern, long pastern, sesamoid, cannon," she began, reeling them off like a pro. When she finished, she could see that the examiner was grinning. Maybe it was because her friends were still standing there, but they weren't standing there quietly. They were clapping like mad.

"Your cheering section seems pleased . . ." the examiner said.

Stevie held her breath for the rest of the sentence.

". . . and so am I."

"Thanks," Stevie said. She stood up and reached for Topside's reins to take him back to his stall.

"Not quite yet," the examiner said. "There are a few more things . . ."

"I CAN'T BELIEVE how much stuff we have to know," Lisa said, watching the rest of Stevie's test from the edge of the ring. Stevie was the only rider trying for D-3. Lisa had been among many who had been tested for D-1. She was pretty sure she'd passed. She'd find out later when Max awarded the ratings to all of the riders. Stevie and Carole had urged her to go for D-2, but that, like earning a horse of her own, would come in time. Lisa was, above all, sensible. She knew it would be a mistake for her to rush herself—even if her parents tried to do it for her!

"Are you nervous?" Lisa asked Carole.

"Of course I am," Carole said. "Anybody with any sense is nervous before a big test and my C-1 rating is a big test. But you guys helped this week—"

"We helped you?" Lisa asked, surprised. "All we did was to get you to drill us on our test material!"

"That helps me. See, everything you're being tested on, I'm already expected to know." It amused Carole to think about how much she actually had learned while teaching her friends. Her father had also drilled her on additional material. She had the feeling he'd picked up a pointer or two along the way.

"Thank you very much, Stevie," the examiner said. "You can take Topside back to his stall now." Stevie walked Topside back into the stable. As she passed her friends, she winked and said "Whew!" They both knew exactly what she meant!

"The C-1 candidate," the examiner announced. "Are you ready?"

"Five minutes!" Carole said. "Just have to tighten my horse's girth and bring him out."

"See that you do," the examiner said. Lisa didn't like his tone of voice at all, but if it bothered Carole, her friend didn't say anything. As Lisa knew, when it came to horses, Carole was all business. Mostly.

As soon as Carole's rating test was over, Max called all of the riders into his office. It was time to find out how they'd done. Some, like Lisa, who had chosen a rating they knew they could pass, were feeling confident. Others, like Stevie and Carole, who thought they might have been reaching beyond their grasp, were more than a little nervous. The look on Max's face told them nothing.

Carole was actually very nervous. Barq had refused a low jump and she was sure that would count against her, even though it was because he'd been startled by a rabbit. It still shouldn't have happened. Then, Carole was sure she'd gotten confused on the veterinary section when the examiner started asking her about parasites. She couldn't, for the life of her, remember where botflies laid their eggs. Her answer, "In their bot-caves?" got an amused response from nearby listeners. She'd also mixed up poultice bandages and cold-water bandages. She was sure she'd failed.

Carole had enough confidence in herself to know that she would certainly pass the test eventually. She'd try again at the next rating, but until then, if she failed, she'd be unrated. Carole looked at the pile of yellow patches on Max's desk, ready to be handed out. D-level Pony Clubbers got to wear yellow patches behind their pins. Carole had been trying for a green. There were no green patches on Max's desk.

"This is going to be fun," Max said, beginning the awards ceremony at last. "It's going to be fun because, I'm pleased to say, all those of you who took D-level tests passed!"

Carole was sitting between her two best friends. She reached a hand out to congratulate each of them. It was no surprise that Lisa had passed. It was a bit of a relief that Stevie had. Her friends each grasped her hand in return.

"I'll be fine," she whispered to them. "I just attempted too much. No problem. I'll try again."

While Carole tried to control the roller-coaster feeling that had just come over her, Max handed out the yellow patches, announcing each Pony Clubber's name and rating as he did. Most of the Horse Wise members took their pins off and installed their patches right away. Stevie and Lisa didn't. Carole was touched by their loyalty.

"Now," Max began again when all the yellow patches had been distributed. "Only one person here felt she was horse wise enough to attempt a C-level rating, and that person, as you know, is Carole Hanson."

Oh, no! Carole thought. Everybody else in the room had passed their tests. She hadn't. And now Max thought he could make it better by giving a talk on noble attempts. She wanted to sink into the floor and reappear in a different county—preferably in a different universe!

". . . the C levels are tough tests. The examiners can't give much leeway. Either the candidate knows her material, or she doesn't."

Even worse, he was dragging it out. Carole couldn't believe Max would do this to her.

"And, in the case of Carole Hanson, I'm pleased to tell you, she *does* know her stuff! Carole, come get your green patch. Congratulations!"

Had she heard right? Her friends nudged her hard. That must mean something, she realized. She stood up and walked toward Max, almost in a trance.

"You mean botflies *do* lay their eggs in botcaves?" Carole asked. Everybody laughed, even Max.

"No, they don't," he said. "They actually lay their eggs on the horse's underside, but you got half credit for creativity on that one!"

He handed her her green patch. Carole accepted it in a happy daze. She wasn't even sure how she got back to her seat. She was too excited to be aware of mundane things like that.

"Now, there's one more award," Max continued. "It's not exactly covered by the U.S. Pony Club regulations, but there are times when exceptions are called for. Besides, this can be a local award. There's one more member of our club who has made an exceptional contribution, over the past few weeks, and who has set an example on how to become horse wise. Can you all guess who is going to get the final yellow patch of the day?"

Carole knew a cue when she heard one. She stood up again and turned to all her friends in Horse Wise. "I think the man is talking about my dad, don't you agree?"

They did. There was a big round of applause, and an embarrassed Colonel Hanson stepped forward.

Max handed Carole the yellow patch. "Will you do the honors?" he asked.

Carole turned to her dad. She'd seen him receive ribbons and pins many times in the Marine Corps. She knew just what to do. As he stood absolutely still, she pinned the patch on his shirt, then saluted him. He returned the salute sharply. Then she hugged him. He returned that, too. That wasn't exactly part of the Marine Corps procedure, but he deserved it.

Once again, Carole returned to her place with her friends. "Saddle Club meeting at TD's right after this?" she whispered. Stevie and Lisa nodded. There was a lot to talk about.

"I'm almost done now," Max said. "There's one more thing I need to talk about, but I don't really like talking about it at all. If this were a stable matter, I wouldn't say anything, but it's a Horse Wise matter and you all deserve to know."

The Saddle Club looked at one another. What was *this* about?

"Last week, one of our members did something very careless—something no Horse Wise person should ever do. She took a horse into the fields and failed to close gates behind her. As a result, Samson, the colt, got into a treacherous situation, saved only by the quick thinking and able attention of three of our members. The Pony Club regulations allow me some latitude on membership requirements. One of them is horse safety. The member who failed to close the gates has been suspended from Horse Wise for a month. The same would happen to anyone who did something so careless, whether it resulted in damage or not."

Carole looked around the room. She could see that everybody was doing the same thing. She heard one Pony Club member ask another, "Who's missing?" Carole grinned. She and her friends didn't have to ask. It was Veronica. For once in her life—in *their* lives—Veronica was getting properly rewarded for her behavior!

Stevie leaned over to whisper to Carole. "This won't be an ordinary Saddle Club meeting," she said. "This will be a Saddle Club quadruple celebration!"

"Quadruple?" Carole asked.

"Sure. One for each of our patches. And one for Veronica!"

14

"Now, let me see if I've got this straight," the waitress at TD's said. Lisa tried to suppress a smile. Eating ice cream with Stevie had its moments.

"You want hot fudge on vanilla," she said to Lisa. Lisa nodded. She turned to Carole. "And you're having a dish of maple walnut?"

"Yes, please," Carole said.

"And yours," she looked at Stevie over her glasses, "is pineapple chunk on bubble-gum-baby ice cream."

"That's right, and could you put some of that marshmallow goo and a cherry on top?"

A look of terror crossed the woman's face. "I don't know," she said, paling. "I'll ask the chef." She fled from their table, but Lisa didn't think she was out of earshot when they all burst into giggles.

"New woman," Carole said.

"But not for long, I fear." Stevie sighed dramatically. They laughed again.

"Oh, I feel so good," Carole said. "It's a kind of all-over wonderful feeling."

"I know just what you mean," Stevie agreed.

"Me, too," Lisa added. "I'm really glad for both of you, passing your advanced ratings. For me and for now, D-1 is enough."

"Actually, although I'm really glad about my D-3, I think I'm really happier about Veronica getting her just desserts."

"Think she'll learn anything from it?" Lisa asked.

"Maybe, maybe not," Carole said. "She's not a fast learner when it comes to her own faults."

"We, on the other hand, are very fast learners, especially when it comes to horses," Lisa said.

"And science projects," Stevie added. "I handed mine in this week, you know, the radish one. I think the teacher liked it, except for the part where I started watering the pots that weren't supposed to get water because I felt so sorry for those poor seeds. They needed water just like I need my—"

"Here you go, girls." The waitress had come back with their orders.

"—sundae," Stevie finished her sentence.

The dishes were on the table and the waitress disappeared before the girls could thank her.

"I think she wanted to get away from Stevie's order," Lisa said.

"She'll learn," Stevie said, taking her first bite. "It's positively delicious."

Her friends didn't believe her, either.

"What were we talking about?" Stevie asked.

"Veronica, of course," Lisa reminded her. "And whether she would ever learn anything."

"The answer to that is probably no," Carole said. "But who cares about her? We're learning and that's the important thing."

"Boy, are we ever!" Stevie said. "I mean, I learned all about horses' leg bones this week. Didn't think I'd ever know that stuff—didn't think I'd ever need to."

"Leg bones are easy," Carole teased. "Wait until you study up on botflies!"

"Oh, yeah, laying their eggs in botcaves. I loved that," Stevie said, giggling. Carole and Lisa laughed as well.

"You're not the only one who's learning," Lisa said, a little bit more seriously. "I learned that I should trust my friends. When I've got trouble, they won't waste time on dumb things like envy. My friends get right down to the important thing—being friends."

The girls looked at one another, feeling the warmth of the moment and the importance of their friendship.

"Looks like there's been a lot of learning going on," Stevie said, scraping the last of the marsh-

mallow goo from the side of her dish. "What I figure it amounts to is that we're all becoming horse
wise!"

Lisa laughed. "You can say that again," she said.

Stevie didn't hesitate. "What I figure it amounts
to is that—"

Lisa turned to Carole. "Good," she said. "We've
found a way to keep her busy, repeating herself. It's
the opportunity we've been waiting for to get a
taste of her delicious sundae!"

Stevie parried their advances on her sundae with
her spoon. "Horse wise, we can do together," she
said. "Sundae wise you can do on your own al-
lowances!"

They all laughed together. It felt very good.

ABOUT THE AUTHOR

BONNIE BRYANT is the author of more than sixty books for young readers, including novelizations of movie hits such as *Teenage Mutant Ninja Turtles®* and *Honey, I Blew Up the Kid,* written under her married name, B. B. Hiller.

Ms. Bryant began writing The Saddle Club in 1986. Although she had done some riding before that, she intensified her studies then and found herself learning right along with her characters Stevie, Carole, and Lisa. She claims that they are all much better riders than she is.

Ms. Bryant was born and raised in New York City. She lives in Greenwich Village with her two sons.